The Quiet Order

I0543837

A mystery about memory,
control,
and what we choose to forget.

Estelle Hartley

Farbellum Press

The Quiet Order
© 2025 Estelle Hartley
All rights reserved.

This is a work of fiction. Names, characters, places, and incidents are the product of the author's imagination or are used fictitiously. Any resemblance to actual events, locales, or persons, living or dead, is entirely coincidental.

Published by Farbellum Press
www.farbellum.com

ISBNs:

978-1-7641306-5-3 (Paperback)

978-1-7641306-6-0 (Ebook)

First edition, 2025

Cover image © Kamil Feczkó, used under license from CoverJig
Cover design by David, Farbellum Press

To the ones who keep asking,

even when the answers are uncomfortable.

She jammed the key into the lock and pushed the door open the moment it clicked. No pause, no breath—just the rush of coming home.

Claire tossed her scarf into the corner, her oversized jacket following behind in a lazy arc. But before she could even sigh, she heard it: the soft scurry of judgment.

Too late. She'd been spotted.

It stared at her from across the room, blinking with feline condescension.
Meow.

"Oh be quiet, Eggroll," she muttered. "I just got home."

The cat, deeply wounded by the accusation, as if Claire had written a fourteen-page dissertation on his impatience.

Trying her best to ignore Eggroll's persistence, she hurried over to her desktop PC, clicking it out of sleep mode to the familiar soft glow and mechanical whirr, all while battling to remove her boots using nothing but sheer will and one hand.

Work was over. Now came the good part; *her* work.

Flicking her chestnut-brown hair back behind her left ear, she adjusted her glasses ever so slightly; eyes wide at the screen as she hummed some tune she'd heard on the subway that morning.

She clicked open a web browser that automatically launched her fourteen regular news and social media tabs at once; a slideshow of information she was keen to delve into.

On the right-hand monitor, a familiar presence appeared, or rather, a friendly line of text.

Her personal AI: Ada.
Hello, the word blinked onscreen, the standard message it displayed when the PC was brought out of sleep.

"Hello," Claire said aloud, just out of habit, even though the microphone wasn't on. She typed it in afterward.

Meow. Eggroll leaped into her lap, reasserting his dominance over her time and attention. Claire cradled him affectionately as she moved to the cupboard to help him select tonight's dinner.

"Now, what's this one? Seafood Delight. Ooh Or do you want just tuna?"
Eggroll meowed.
"Tuna it is. Honestly, Eggroll, I think Seafood Delight is just code for whatever they dragged up in the net. We may need to reconsider our buying choices in future, based on their no-doubt nefarious fishing practices."

She smirked, opening the tin and emptying the contents into Eggroll's bowl.

With that out of the way, the cat disengaged hastily gorging on the tuna feast, then sitting quite content afterward, licking his paws and watching a small moth that had slipped in with Claire before. The Norwood apartment she lived in might have been on the fifth floor, up several old staircases, but somehow, even here, nature found a way to rise above the hum.

As she reached for her mug, her gaze flicked briefly to the hallway mirror across the room.

Something about it gave her pause.

For a moment, just a split second, she thought she saw someone else's reflection standing behind her. Not moving. Just there.

Her breath caught. She turned.

Nothing.

Just the old radiator. A half-folded blanket on the chair. Eggroll, staring up at her, utterly unbothered.

Claire blinked, heart thudding louder than she liked to admit. "Okay," she whispered, shaking her head. "Okay."

She returned to her seat, telling herself it was just the city lights playing tricks. Still, she found herself dragging the curtain half-closed behind her.

Back at the PC, Claire set down a newly made cup of peppermint tea, its steam lazily rising in front of her glasses as she clicked through her tabs, reading, absorbing.

Claire was no doomscroller. Her interest in the news came from watching the trends, reading between the lines, finding the real stories, and going down rabbit holes. It was a passionate pastime and allowed her mind to wander, sometimes too far; but it always rewarded her with what she sought: more knowledge.

As she went on, she would insert passages into Ada, asking for clarification or prompting Ada to find related sources. Ada was Claire's scrolling right hand; always ready for some text-based adventure.

On this occasion, her evening fun was interrupted by darkness; the room still lit faintly from the soft glow of New York City filtering in through the window. Claire didn't react with fear. In this ageing apartment block, it was a weekly occurrence usually ending with the superintendent descending into the basement with an assortment of tools that seemed more suited to plumbing than electrical work.

She didn't fault him; the power always came back on; no doubt at significant risk to his livelihood.

While the power was out, she slid a dining chair close to the fogged window and cracked it open, trying to remember the German word for exchanging the air in a house. "Fluschehgugen," she said aloud, giggling to herself, almost instinctively turning to type it into Ada before remembering the power was out.

Eggroll, having completed his personal VIP grooming session, did not miss the opportunity.
As Claire pulled the chair toward the window and sat down, starting to relax, he leapt onto her lap with a small meow followed by a purr loud enough to rival a jumbo jet engine.

Claire glanced at the street below: the evening hum, the sound of distant horns, a homeless man pushing a trolley, a police cruiser speeding past, the rattle of a trash can lid being closed, and muted shouting from a neighbour who seemed to be coping poorly with the electricity outage.

She loved this city. Loved feeling it, watching it.

The next morning, Claire awoke with a start. A strange, furry creature seemed intent on trying to suffocate her in her sleep.

Pushing Eggroll off her face, she stumbled toward the bathroom, lazily starting the shower.

Ten minutes later, she was ready. Always a minimalist, the makeup commercials and beauty regimens on TikTok bounced off her like Teflon.

She was naturally beautiful. But unlike many of her peers in New York City, she didn't feel the need to layer that beauty to meet anyone's expectations.

It wasn't that she didn't care about her appearance; it's that she cared just enough.

The morning sun coming through the window glinted off her simple necklace: a silver chain holding her mother's wedding ring. Claire never left home without it. A reminder of a mother with a brilliant soul and a childhood full of riverside fishing, snowball fights in winter, camping in state parks, and being generally mischievous.

Norwood had an unpretentious beauty about it in parts. Little pockets that hadn't yet been gentrified still marked with the grime of a city that never slept. Small slivers of the New York of old.

Catching the subway was a routine for Claire, just another part of her day made less mundane by the way her mind worked. Technically, she could take the bus or even cycle from Norwood to Fordham University, where she worked in the Bronx.
But the subway *hummed*... and once you got used to the smell, well, it was New York, after all.

During the morning rush, Claire generally stood, but she used the time to study others. Not too intently, never in a way that might attract unwanted attention or give any man the wrong idea.
To her, they were like browser tabs: glanced at from the side, glimpses of patterns, hints of the stories underneath.
It was a game she played trying to guess who they were, how they lived, what they were doing.

Some were easier than others. The businessmen always seemed a little hollow to her. Not because *they* were hollow, but because their clothing lacked expression; as if the corporate world had, ever so subtly, scraped off a layer of who they were supposed to be.

The kids always interested her; their changing fashions, their muttered slang, the rotating carousel of new apps and in-jokes. They were, in a way, a barometer of what the world considered "cool," recalibrated every few months.

Claire was thirty-five. Like many in her generation, she had never married and had no children. It wasn't a deliberate choice. For Claire, life had simply turned out that way, and had never paused long enough to question it.
Perhaps, deep down, it had something to do with losing her parents at such a young age.

She always joked that she'd adopt two hundred cats and become a crazy cat lady in her old age, if only to annoy Eggroll.

People pushed past her, jostled, glanced, read books; most stared at their phones. Claire studied them. Never with judgment and always in passing.

Once at Fordham University, she made her way to her office on the fourth floor of the William D. Walsh Family Library. It was a small, nondescript room; someone had jokingly stuck an A4 piece of paper to the door with "Claire's Office of Resurrection" scrawled across it.

Among her fellow archivists, she had developed a reputation: the one who could handle the strangest forms of media, develop new systems for cataloguing, and more than anything *find* things.

Technically, Claire was still a freelancer. Even after two years, she remained contracted. but she didn't mind. She understood it was more a reflection of university budgets than of her abilities.

And to the rest of the staff, she was family.

Not long after sitting down, Claire idly touched the ring on her necklace, sliding it back and forth out of habit as she powered on her office PC.

There was a sharp rap at the door, and before she could respond, Citra burst in clearly operating on more caffeine than should be legal, even in a city like New York.

"Claire! Claire! Did you see the article on me?" Citra grinned, shoving a copy of the university paper toward her. "Oh my god they printed it!"

"And who would've thought the real press cares about the quiet, diligent work of archivists like you," Claire replied warmly, smiling back.

"Yes! Okay, the article oh my god, it's so boring *but* hear me out: I can use it for my CV! Like, as a portfolio thing for when I apply for other jobs!"
Citra bounced on the spot, practically vibrating.

"I'm so proud of you, Citra. You've worked so hard this last year. Just watch out. If archival jealousy is a real thing, you're about to be the target."

"What are they going to do, huh?" Citra said with mock defiance. "Mislabel the Dewey system in the whole library to confuse me?"

Their work at the university varied depending on their roles. Claire, as a digital archivist, handled digital-born materials like PDFs, photos, and websites. Citra, on the other hand, was a reference archivist: her job was to help students and faculty locate the information they needed. She had arrived a year ago on a work visa from Indonesia and, quickly, she and Claire had developed a close friendship.

Citra's skillset went far beyond archiving. Like many migrants, she was multi-skilled with a strong background in IT, particularly programming and AI systems.
A few months after they had met, Citra had presented Claire with the perfect gift: Ada.

Ada was a locally based AI, designed to specialize in search and referencing. Ada had become an invaluable tool in Claire's quest to uncover the unseen threads behind the information she consumed.

She was forever thankful to Citra for sharing her invention. As far as Claire knew, only the two of them had a working version. Sure, in an age of technological rapidity, there were other options out there but the connection to Citra made Ada special. Like a handcrafted item from a pottery studio, it carried her mark.

Most weekends especially Saturdays, Claire and Citra were inseparable.

Despite her passion for information, Claire made a point of clawing herself away from the apartment each week, much to Eggroll's disappointment, and spending the day with Citra.

Sometimes it was a theatre performance; other times, the cinema or a walk-through Central Park. But always, there was laughter.

In the past year, Citra's dating life had also become a significant source of amusement. Claire found no shortage of entertainment in the strange ritual of modern courtship, which appeared to revolve largely around swiping left or right on a glowing rectangle.

It had never appealed to Claire.

Sure, there were pangs of loneliness now and then, and she'd had relationships here and there.

But none of them had risen to the level where marriage felt like a serious option. She had never experienced that sense of *need* for another person.

It was, in its own way, both a burden and a relief. Sometimes she wished she had that need; it might have made things simpler, easier to settle down.

Other times, when she heard about Citra's dating

misadventures, she felt almost smug in her solitude; content to be exactly where she was.

The day wore on: cataloguing, marking, describing. There was nothing glamorous in the work, but its predictability gave Claire a certain comfort.

By evening, Claire once again stood outside her apartment door, key in hand, but just before it turned, her phone rang.
She glanced at the screen. A number she didn't recognise, but the area code stopped her: Ashridge.

Answering, she said simply, "Hello?"

"Oh hello, is that Claire? Claire Halstead?"

"Yes," she replied, opening her door with her free hand and setting down her scarf and jacket on the floor. Eggroll gave her a disapproving glance, annoyed at her delay in greeting.

"I'm so sorry to tell you this. Oh. I should start with who I am. This is Janine Baskill. I'm the on-duty manager at the Shadeston Retirement Facility here in Ashridge Hollow. Are you Claire Halstead, relative of Dr. Malcolm Halstead?"

Claire paused.

Her uncle. Uncle Malcolm.
She hadn't seen him since she was seventeen. So many years ago; but she could still picture his chubby face

and overgrown moustache, as if it were fighting to claim its own zip code in real estate across his cheeks.

He had always been a jovial presence during her childhood: turning up at birthdays, offering encouragement, but never embedded in the daily rhythm of her life. Like most extended family, he was a Christmas presence, not a long-weekend one.

"Uh-huh," she answered.

"I didn't want to be the one to tell you. I've only just started here; but I'm sorry, your uncle, Dr. Halstead, passed away this afternoon. He died peacefully in his sleep. You were listed as his emergency contact."

"Malcolm..." she said under her breath. "I haven't seen him in years. Are you sure you meant to call me?"

"Yes, Claire. You were the only family member he listed. He's been with us here for just under two years now. You didn't know?"

"No, no... we lost touch some time ago."

The manager's voice didn't waver. "That's okay. It happens a lot with family as people get older. I'm sorry to burden you, but since you were listed as his emergency contact, we have his belongings here for you to collect when you can. We need to prepare his room for someone else."

16

She paused then, perhaps realising how clinical it all sounded then closed with a few polite condolences and hung up.

Her solemn duty complete.

Claire turned slowly, instinctively running her hand over the keyboard to wake the screen. Ada blinked to life on the right-hand monitor; tabs still glowed quietly on the left.

Stunned by the call, but carried forward by habit, Claire opened a tin for Eggroll, then slumped into her chair no tea this time. She sat in silence, trying to make sense of it.

It's been years... why would he list me?

She closed all the preloaded tabs and opened a few search engines, typing in: *Dr. Malcolm Halstead.*

She knew who he was at least, in the family sense. But this was her way of entering grief: a slow reintroduction to who he had become.

She scanned the pages, the accolades, the archived interviews.

Dr. Malcolm Halstead was a respected cultural anthropologist, best known for his work on modern systems and institutional behaviour; from government agencies to early online communities.
His research explored how belief, power, and identity

were shaped not in remote tribes, but in ordinary structures: school boards, office hierarchies, digital forums.

He was known for treating bureaucracy itself as a kind of ritual performance; one filled with its own myths, taboos, and invisible rules.

Claire stood at the photocopier, staring at the blinking light as if it might offer wisdom. Behind her, the office buzzed in that semi-quiet way archives always did; a few keyboards tapping, someone coughing twice too loudly, the rhythmic creak of a chair that had survived too many grant cycles.

Citra peeked her head in, carrying two overfilled takeaway coffees like a chaotic offering.
"One day," she said, "they will invent lids that don't leak if you breathe near them."

Claire smiled faintly, taking one.
"How do you always time your entrances with my existential moments?"

"It's a gift," Citra replied, leaning against the filing cabinet. "So. What's up? You've been staring at that copier like it insulted your mother."

Claire hesitated, then sighed.
"I need to take a few days off. Maybe a week."

Citra tilted her head. "Everything okay?"

"You remember I told you about my uncle? Malcolm?"

"The one who studied office politics like it was an ancient religion?"

"That's the one," Claire said. "He passed away. I got a call from the nursing home. I was listed as his emergency contact."

Citra's expression softened; she reached out and gave Claire a light hug.
"Claire. I'm so sorry."

Claire gave a small shrug. "Thanks. I hadn't seen him in years. But, I'm the only surviving family, so… I have to head back to Ashridge Hollow. Sort through his things. Handle the estate. Whatever that means."

Citra nodded, the humour briefly leaving her voice. "That's a lot."

"Yeah."

There was a pause, filled only by the copier finally coming to life with a groan.

Then: "Want me to look after Eggroll?"

Claire blinked. "You'd really do that?"

"Please. I've been waiting for my shot at winning him over. This is the longest slow-burn enemies-to-lovers arc of my life."

Claire laughed.

"He's going to manipulate you within twenty-four hours. He pretends to starve if there's less than seven biscuits in the bowl."

"I'll fall for it. I'm weak. But I'll live. You may come back to Eggroll being twice as large."

Claire took a sip of coffee.
"You're a good friend."

Citra waved it off.

"It's mutual. Just don't forget to load Ada onto your laptop before you go. You'll miss her more than me."

"I already copied her local files," Claire said, grinning at the fact Citra could read her so easily. "Though I swear she's sulking about being moved."

"She does get emotionally attached to the apartment. And Eggroll," Citra said, mock-serious. "Classic co-dependency."

They stood in silence a beat longer.

"You sure you're okay to do this alone?" Citra asked gently.

Claire nodded.
"Yeah. I think I need to."

A few days later, Claire stood outside the Shadeston Retirement Facility, unsure what exactly she was supposed to feel.

The building looked like every other aged care home she'd ever seen: bland siding, low hedges, and a bench that hadn't been sat on in so long it had started to gather dust.

An ambulance was parked at the side entrance; an all-too-familiar sight at aged care facilities, another soul having quietly succumbed to the whimsy of mortality.

She glanced at the door, reached out... and hesitated.

Inside, after signing several documents, the woman at the front desk handed her a worn canvas bag, the kind that looked more like a laundry sack than luggage, and a manila envelope clipped shut. A single house key was taped to the outside.

"He kept to himself. Except if there was a puzzle," the woman said, smiling gently.
"He had this thing about stealing pieces from other people's boxes. Thought it was funny."

She gave a light shrug. "Polite man. Definitely a night owl."

21

The adjacent staff member sat quietly, appearing busy with a notepad. Claire glanced over as if something about them tugged at her memory.

It wasn't the face; it was the feeling. For a moment, it seemed like they were listening, not writing.

Then they looked up. Their eyes locked with Claire's just for a second before flicking away quickly.

Was that guilt? she wondered. What was that?

The cab pulled away, tires crunching over gravel, leaving Claire alone at the edge of the driveway.

The house stood still against a backdrop of tall, leafless trees; a single-story colonial with grey-blue clapboard siding faded by decades of sun and snow. The shutters were crooked, one hanging loose like it had given up. Moss grew in the cracks of the stone steps. The porch sagged slightly in the middle, as if tired of waiting for company.

There was a single porch light, yellowed with age, still working. Someone had left it on.

A wind chime tinkled faintly, though there was no wind.

Above the door, an old iron number plate: 128. The font was elegant but felt out of place.

Claire hesitated at the door. The key in her hand felt suddenly small.

The kind of key that opened not just doors, but memories.

Claire touched her necklace instinctively with her other hand.

She stepped onto the porch, the wood giving slightly under her boots.

For a moment, she pictured him there with mug in hand, watching the street with that quiet patience of his and that friendly smile.

It hurt more than she expected.

Opening the door, dust swirled from the floorboards as if time itself had been reawakened; light filtered in and struck a myriad of objects lining the walls. Her uncle had been an avid collector; of the old, the odd, and the inexplicable.

She ran her hand along the nearest bench. Dust trickled down in soft little plumes as she scanned the items.

A number plate here. An inkwell there. A signed football. What looked like early-model Pez dispensers.

The first few shelves after the entrance seemed almost designed to confuse visitors with a calculated scattering of curiosities, giving off so many different impressions that it became impossible to pin the owner down. Hobbies, interests, affiliations; all blurred.

Turning left into the first room, she entered the lounge. The moment she crossed the threshold; it was as if someone had transported her back in time.

In the corner, dominating the room with its sheer size, was an old CRT television on its original inbuilt black stand. The exact same model Claire remembered from her childhood.

A DVD player sat below it. Claire tried to recall the last time she'd seen one. Her cataloguing mind noted, absently, that the DVD player was over fifteen years newer than the television.

A two-seater brown leather couch and a single recliner sat against the far wall, angled toward the window with the television off to the right.

Why were living rooms always set up like that?

Oh, right. It was from an age when the screen was part of the space... but not yet the whole point of it.

She smiled at the thought.

Eggroll would love this place; exploring it like some ancient archaeologist, trying to figure out how the humans used to live.

Slam!

The breeze caught the door, making Claire startle and spin around, half-expecting to see someone standing there in the hallway. A shiver ran up her spine.

"Stop crossing my grave, Uncle. I'm just here to get things wrapped up for you, I promise," she said to no one in particular.

As if in response, a crow outside let out a rough squawk, its sound carrying softly through the old windowpane.

With the lounge room behind her, Claire moved on. Not quite confidently, but with a quiet sense of purpose and fragility. She was aware of the life that had once inhabited these walls, and of the great mind that had moved within them.

Next came the kitchen and dining area, to the right: a spotless stovetop. Not because it had been kept particularly clean, but because Malcolm hadn't really cooked. He grazed, he assembled, he reheated, but cooking? That required the kind of focus he reserved entirely for his research.

A row of spice jars sat untouched in a wire rack, their labels still crisp as if they'd been bought together in a set and never once opened. The oven door was slightly ajar, as though it had never quite closed properly but no one had bothered to fix it. A note in Malcolm's handwriting was stuck to the inside of a cupboard: "Do not boil eggs in the electric kettle again." Claire blinked, unsure if it was a warning to himself or the ghost of some earlier domestic experiment.

The microwave sat quietly in the corner, its clock forever blinking 12:00.

She paused in front of the spice rack for a moment. "Never opened," she murmured. "Catalogued."
Then moved on.

Malcolm had never married, had chosen solitude over a family, but he had still found time to bring joy to the people around him. In a strange way, his cluttered systems and forgotten kitchen habits reminded Claire of her own. The passion he'd poured into his university work had left little room for things like recipes or dinner parties.

Perhaps that was it. In some ways, everyone had been family to Malcolm, back when he was younger.
Before the dementia.
Before Claire's own life had changed so suddenly with the death of her parents.

The kitchen was neat at first glance, but the benches were piled high with unopened envelopes. It was as if Malcolm had spent his final months performing an anthropological experiment on the ritual of mail. A sign of a mind slowly fading, yet still holding so much it wanted to give.

There was regret in that moment. Regret that she hadn't come sooner. She remembered why. She *had* wanted to, but back then it would've meant facing her grief all over again. The loss of her parents at seventeen had taken years of therapy to process, years to turn that pain into something like memory instead of rawness.

She forced the thought aside and shuffled through the mail.

Electricity bills. A National Geographic subscription. Countless pieces of junk mail. Several advertisements offering new credit cards; the American punishment for maintaining a good credit score.

One envelope caught her attention. Handwritten. Unopened. Her analytical mind scanned the postmark, dated around two years ago. Just a few months before Malcolm had entered the nursing facility.

She turned it over slowly. No return address.

After a moment's hesitation, curiosity won. She ran her fingernail carefully along the seal and removed a single letter, folded neatly into four.

Dr. Halstead,

I waited as long as I could, but I think I've found it. Not the whole picture, not yet. But there's something that doesn't fit.

It was exactly where you said it might be, buried under all that local history they pretend not to remember. Took some sweet-talking and a few late nights, but I managed to get my hands on the records.

You were right. The dates don't line up, and the name appears more than once, in places it shouldn't. Someone went to a lot of effort to make sure it all stayed buried.

I know you said not to write, but I had to tell you. If anything happens, if someone else comes don't talk to them Malcolm.

Take care of yourself, Mal. You always said the truth had patterns. I think you were closer to one than you realised.

C. Weaver

Another shiver ran up Claire's spine as she finished reading.

Patterns.

Claire didn't just like patterns, she *saw* the world through them. It was how she made sense of chaos. But this... this didn't make sense yet.
What place were they talking about?
Was the letter a prank?

She examined it again, slowly. Tried to think rationally about who her uncle was. Maybe the early stages of dementia had led him into some half-baked wild goose chase?

No. That didn't explain someone else joining in. That didn't explain the letter.
There was more to this.

This was a mystery her pattern-seeking mind couldn't solve. Not yet. Not with a single letter.
She ran her fingernail across the signature. *C. Weaver.*

Gently, she folded the letter again and slipped it back into the envelope, then into her backpack alongside her laptop.

She moved on through the house, the quietness pressing against her; and then, almost involuntarily, let out a small laugh.

Scooby-Doo.

It had been one of her favourite cartoons growing up. And now, somehow, she'd stumbled onto a real mystery. A mystery that didn't involve masks or theme parks, but something that still beckoned her, like a siren calls a sailor.

Turning to the kettle, she lifted it and opened the lid half-expecting, for some reason, to find a dozen eggs inside.
Pleased it was empty, Claire walked over to the sink, filled it up, and plugged it back in.

Whilst the kitchen filled with the gentle hum of the kettle, she opened three tea tins until she found what she was looking for: peppermint tea.
It had been her uncle who introduced her to it when she was a teenager. Something that, years later, would become trendy but to her, it was just warm comfort.

Despite the tea bag's age and faint loss of scent, she removed one, placing it gently into a white mug with "I Came. I Dug. I Catalogued" written on it.

Sitting at the table and giving the tea a moment, she looked out the kitchen window. The sugar maple tree dominated the view with a peaceful kind of charm, its leaves still green despite the slight drop in the air that hinted at a coming autumn. An old clothesline rattled.

No visible houses behind the fence line. Just a view of forest and *adventure*.

As a child, those forests Claire knew well, taking her father's four-wheeler out as a teenager to explore with her close group of friends.
She had always preferred the open country to the party scene. More likely to be found fishing or camping than drinking beer through a funnel, terribly quick.
Her childhood friends could be counted on two hands. But those friendships were worth a thousand acquaintances.

Still staring at the sugar maple tree, Claire allowed herself a moment of memory.

The moment.
Memory as clear as if it were yesterday.

She wasn't home at the time.
In class during her senior year in English Literature,
one of her favourite lessons. Her notepad doodled
with crooked love hearts and warm scribbles from
friends, open on her desk.

The teacher was talking about the novel *Mrs Dalloway*
by Virginia Woolf. With her soft, canonical voice, she
had remarked:

"She always had the feeling that it was very, very
dangerous to live even one day."

At that moment, through the windowed doorway, two
local policemen entered.
No one was alarmed; everyone knew the police in
Ashridge Hollow. It was Tom Granger and Rick
Donnelly. They spent most of their time chasing after
teenagers having get-togethers in the forest, following
up on noise complaints or dealing with speeding traffic.

They looked over at Claire, then back to the teacher.
Walked toward her desk, removed their caps, and held

them in their hands.
One leaned in. Whispered something.

Claire could still remember gripping the ballpoint pen tighter and tighter as they approached, her heart sinking in that moment of suspended, sickening uncertainty before they led her outside and gave her the news.

What happens when a seventeen-year-old learns that both her parents, her only close family have died, and with it had her world irrevocably shattered?
Everything happens.
Every stage of grief, all at once. Then again. And again.

Snapping herself out of the moment, she stared down at the peppermint tea.
Lifting the mug, she took a few sips before standing up, shaking off the weight of it.

Claire had learned a kind of resilience most people never need to.
Years of navigating her own trauma had given her the ability to catalogue and shelve her emotions when needed. Not in a cruel, heartless way, but in a way that was kind to her soul.
A way that let her return to those memories when the time was right.

The sun lazily stretched across the sink as she reached for a cloth, rinsed the cup, and returned it to the cupboard. Needing something to focus on, Claire opened a few drawers; aimlessly at first, as if she were the anthropologist now, excavating the lost world of her uncle.

In the bottom drawer beside the sink, she stooped and looked closer, intrigued. The light glinted off the edge of a black leather-bound journal, oddly well-preserved. It was newer than most of the sun-worn, dust-caked objects in the house. That alone was enough to spark her interest.

Standing again, she leaned on the bench and opened the cover with care.

On the first page, drawn by hand with deliberate lines, was a single symbol: a triangle, with the letters "TE" inscribed in its centre.

Nothing spectacular. But her uncle never put pen to paper without reason.

She turned the page: nothing. Blank. As if whoever had marked the first had abandoned the rest, leaving the journal to the fate of so many others: unwritten, unused, forgotten.

But further in, something caught her eye.

Roughly halfway through, a lone page stood out, its ink dense, deliberate. Claire couldn't make sense of it at first, but her instincts stirred. There was structure. Rhythm. Pattern.

Rows of letters and numbers formed a grid-like page. Not random scribbles, but something methodical. Something coded.

A cipher.

Claire had encountered ciphers before in academic texts or dusty dissertations; but they'd never held her interest for long.

Until now.

This one called to her in a way she couldn't explain. Her eyes scanned the rows, trying to will meaning into the shapes. Is that a vowel? A frequency marker? As if sheer focus alone could force the answer to emerge.

On another day, she might have dismissed it. A teenage prank. A puzzle left unfinished.

But not today. Not in this house. Not after that letter.

Something inside her whispered: this mattered.

Without hesitation, Claire crossed to the hallway and grabbed her bag. From it, she pulled her laptop, setting it down on the kitchen table. She placed the letter beside the journal, side by side.

Two questions.
One machine.
Time to begin.

Ada blinked to life on the screen, seemingly content with the transition to a smaller piece of hardware.

Claire typed:
How are you, Ada? Ready to work?

After a short pause, Ada replied:
Sure. Let's go.

There was comfort in the rhythm of it. On a day weighed down by old memories and half-forgotten rooms, the keyboard and Ada grounded Claire. It felt like she was back in her apartment, surrounded by the familiar.

She glanced to the right, half-expecting to see Eggroll curled up on the couch arm. The thought made her smile and imagine poor Citra at home, bracing for Eggroll's silent judgment.

Focus, Claire told herself.

Her fingers flew across the keys with practiced precision. Claire was fast enough to humble a 1950s typing pool. She transcribed the letter word for word into Ada, then added a request for context.

Claire typed:
Ada, I found this letter in my deceased uncle's house. It was unopened but seems important. He lived in Ashridge Hollow where we are now. Note the postmark: Ashridge Hollow. So it was sent locally.
Can you try and ascertain who "C. Weaver" is?

Ada blinked. Then paused longer than before.

Claire glanced at the corner of the screen to confirm her phone's tethered connection was still live.

Ada wasn't psychic.
But when she worked, she was damn good.

A torrent of text appeared too fast to read in real time. Claire often joked that this was Ada's quiet revenge for vague prompts; holding back, then delivering everything at once.

Ada replied:
C. Weaver. Results within 50 miles of Ashridge Hollow:

Chris Weaver, age 5 — resides in Piercefield. Tagged on social media as son of Claire and Steven Weaver.

Cassidy Weaver, age 37 — resides in Piercefield. Occupation: unknown.

Casey Weaver, age 58 — resides in Ashridge Hollow. Occupation: priest.

Claire exhaled, relieved. A far cry from the avalanche she'd get searching around New York City.

Still, doubt nagged her. It could be a transient visitor or a pseudonym. But she trusted this. *Felt* this. One of these was her sender.

Chris is out, she thought with bemusement, *probably busy with Lego.*

She pressed on for clarity.

Claire typed:
Ada, tell me about Cassidy and Casey Weaver. Can you find images, workplace details for Casey, and any further information about Cassidy?

Ada paused, the cursor blinking teasingly, before opening several browser windows tabulated by person.

Claire clicked through methodically:

- *Cassidy's Facebook page:* photos of her and Chris on road trips, a family birthday, and a fluffy dog that would horrify Eggroll.

- *A women's hockey league site:* Cassidy appearing in C-grade rankings. Plain text, a typical hastily set up local sports team page.

- *An occupational profile:* Cassidy pictured hugging a pole beneath a mirror ball, her sun-kissed skin betraying too many tanning sessions.

"So that's your day job," Claire murmured to no one.

She moved on to Casey Weaver:

Ada replied:

On reviewing the information, there is over a ninety-percent chance it was Casey Weaver based on location, age, and occupation.

Tabs revealed:

- An infrequently updated Facebook profile.

- A Reddit account seeking DIY tips.

- Four religious forum sites where Casey posted as *DustAndGrace* offering sermon advice and existential reflections.

He was thoughtful, compassionate, devoted to his parishioners. The perfect match.

Satisfied, Claire typed a brief acknowledgment.

Night fell sooner than expected. The three-seater couch, oddly like new, despite being older than Claire, became a welcome refuge. She felt a support here she hadn't anticipated as if being present in her uncle's house was in itself a step toward closure.

She had dozed off on the couch with a blanket half-draped over her legs, the scent of dust and old wood clinging faintly in the air.

The living room was dim with just the hallway nightlight casting a weak orange glow against the wall.

At some point in the early hours, Claire felt herself drifting. Not quite asleep, not fully awake.

Her limbs were heavy. Her breath shallow.

She tried to shift, to turn over, but her body stayed still. Pinned. As if gravity had grown stronger just for her.

That's when she heard it.

The unmistakable sound of the rear sliding door easing open.
A slow creak. Careful. Cautious. Deliberate.

Then a pause.

Her heartbeat surged, but her chest remained frozen. She couldn't lift her head. Couldn't move her hands. Couldn't speak.

Footsteps.
Soft. Slow. Just inside the hallway. Nearer

She wanted to scream, to kick, to sit up but all she could do was listen as the intruder moved through the entryway. Past the kitchen.

And stopped.

Right behind her.

No breath. No sound. Just the overwhelming sense of someone standing there. Watching.

Claire's eyes fluttered, but even they felt trapped. All she could do was *feel* it; a presence, thick in the air.

And then... silence.

Total silence.

The next morning, Claire woke with a jolt. Limbs tangled in the couch blanket, heart racing, throat dry. For a second, she didn't know where she was.

Not her apartment. No hum of city traffic. No blinking blue light from her desktop PC. Just silence. Wooden walls. A faint draft.

Malcolm's house.

She sat up slowly, the sleep paralysis memory crawling back to her: the pressure on her chest, the helplessness and the sound. That soft creak of the front door. Had she dreamed it?

A sharp breeze met her as she stepped into the kitchen. The sliding door to the backyard was open ajar by several inches.

Claire froze.

She was sure she'd closed it.

Her eyes scanned the room, breath held. The silence felt wrong. Weighted. Listening.

Grabbing the nearest saucepan from the dish rack, she clenched it tight in one hand and tucked her laptop under her arm with the other.
Not exactly a weapon, but it would do.

She moved room to room sweeping the living area, the guest bedroom, the hallway. Checked closets. Under beds. Behind the shower curtain. Nothing. But she checked again anyway.

Back in the kitchen, she locked the sliding door and paused.

The drawer where she'd found Malcolm's journal was slightly open.

Her stomach dropped.

Someone had been looking. For what?

She glanced at the laptop. It hadn't been touched.

Should I call the police?

She played the scenario in her head "Yes, officer, I had sleep paralysis and then a drawer was half open."
Not exactly compelling evidence.

Claire exhaled sharply and shook her head.

Maybe she'd just left the drawer open. Maybe the wind caught the door. Maybe.

She set down the saucepan, clicked on the kettle, and rubbed the sleep from her face as the kitchen floor creaked softly beneath her feet. Her jeans felt too tight from how she'd slept. Everything felt a little off.

She made her peppermint tea and sat at the table; not sipping yet, just holding it. Staring out through the slightly fogged glass toward the backyard.

Something had happened last night.

But what? Shaking off her thoughts, she took a breather and opened her laptop.

Claire typed:
Ada, do you work with cryptography?

Ada replied almost instantly:
What type specifically? I have working knowledge of substitution ciphers, transposition ciphers, symmetric-key algorithms, and several classical methods. Citra fine-tuned me in this area. I would be delighted to assist.

Claire smiled. *Thanks, Citra,* she thought, before continuing.

Claire typed:
I'm not sure what this is. It looks like some sort of substitution code. maybe old-school. But I've typed it up below, line for line.

She carefully entered the cipher from the journal, making sure to preserve the original formatting.

Ada blinked. Then paused. A long pause of nearly half a minute.

Claire leaned in.

Finally, the reply appeared:

Claire, this is a hybrid cipher. A combination of homophonic substitution and columnar transposition. The original message was encoded using multiple substitutes for common letters then reorganized into columns using a keyword.

Claire typed:
Would someone go to this much effort for a joke? Or just to pass a note between friends?

Ada replied:
Unlikely. This method is historically layered not overly complex by modern standards, but intentional. Homophonic substitution was used during the Renaissance and both World Wars. Combined with columnar transposition, this suggests knowledge of classical encryption techniques.

Claire sipped her tea that now cold and looked out the window at the maple tree. *This wasn't random,* she thought. *Chosen with purpose.*

Claire typed:
Can we try to decode it using "DUSTANDGRACE" as the

keyword? It might be relevant... it's the same phrase a forum user named Casey Weaver used.

Ada blinked again. Then her cursor danced.

Acknowledged. Applying "DUSTANDGRACE" as transposition key... testing homophonic patterns... matching frequency clusters...

A few seconds passed.

Then lines began to appear one after another. They were clear and orderly, as if they'd always been there beneath the surface.

Decrypted Journal Message (as revealed by Ada)

"Some stayed loyal. Some stayed silent. And some… left."

Erased from Order Records:

Elijah Morran – Former Archivist, Northern Chapter

Sarah Flynn – Former Initiate, Southern Wing

Nathaniel Cress – Keeper of Cycles
[status unknown]

Casey Weaver – Interpreter of Signs, (Ashridge Hollow)
[status: Disavowed]

Jonah Hale – No title recorded

Someone wanted them erased. I don't know who.
But I know what that kind of silence means.

This isn't the first version. I threw the others out.
I'm tired of forgetting everything.
It's not finished. I wasn't fast enough.
If it survives, let it mean something.
 MH

Stunned, Claire stared at the screen, trying to absorb both the facts before her and the heartfelt sorrow in her uncle's words. It was the message of a man fighting on the edge of memory loss, desperate to get the truth out while he still could.

And then there was Casey Weaver. His name stood out now, unmistakable. *Interpreter of Signs*; a title heavy with meaning, and suspicion. Six names. Erased. Someone had wanted them gone.

Not in the physical sense, Claire hoped. Maybe about reputations. Prestige. Employment. The quiet kind of deletion she'd seen between the lines of news articles: the language of institutions, of hidden hands and backroom decisions.

But this... this so-called Order was beginning to catch sunlight.

Claire brought the browser tabs back up, scrolling through Casey's forum posts. She wondered if they were coded, or if the others he spoke with were part of the same buried network.

But the language seemed so ordinary.

What she *did* have was a path forward. A name. Casey Weaver. And a church, one she knew well. As a child, she'd been forced to clean there for several weekends after accidentally shattering a stained glass window with a stray rock.

Approaching **St. Luke's Church**, Claire felt the strange blur of past and present. It looked exactly as she remembered it at eleven, chasing Brad through the parking lot with a handful of pebbles.

The church sat just off the main street, near the turnoff for State Route 16. A carefully maintained lawn wrapped around it, bordered by a chest-high wooden fence. Bright white with colonial lines, it stood proud; the steeple tall, the stained glass still glowing even under overcast skies. She could still pick out the very pane she had shattered.

The car park beside the church was empty. It had always been too small, even when she was a child. But on Sundays, no one cared. Cars would line the verge for half a mile, and it was just another piece of small-town life.

A car whizzed past. Two teenagers yelled something indecipherable out the window. Claire pulled her jacket tighter against the cold.

The church door was plain; double doors, unadorned, like a modern replacement added without ceremony. For the first time, she hesitated.

Should I knock?

This was her hometown. She'd grown up in Ashridge Hollow. But after leaving at seventeen, she no longer felt like she had the right to act like a local. Back then, she wouldn't have knocked. Not on a church door.

She knocked.

Knock, knock.

A door creaked open somewhere deep in the building, followed by footsteps. A moment later, the front door groaned open to reveal a man in his fifties; a few inches taller than Claire, thick-lensed reading glasses, a receding hairline, and a kind, slightly worn smile.

It was Casey, just like in the photos.

"Oh! Hello, dear. You're quite a few days early for liturgy. Indeed, by quite a few days!" he said cheerfully. "Let me guess, passing through town? Want to take some pictures of the old place? It's alright, I understand. There aren't many churches like her left," he added, glancing up toward the rafters.

"Oh no," Claire said, offering her hand. "My name's Claire. I just came back to town. I believe you knew my uncle… Malcolm. Malcolm Halstead."

Casey froze. The smile faltered. A more cautious expression took its place as he studied her face.

"Claire, was it? Forgive me if this sounds strange but, in this day, and age, you never know. There are so many fraudsters floating around the internet. How do I know you're really his niece?"

Claire blinked.

This was Ashridge Hollow. Her hometown. A church. And still, she felt like a stranger.

Noticing the silence, "Oh, I'm sorry, my dear. How rude of me. Please, come in." Ushering her inside and closing the door, the priest took a seat on the nearest set of pews and gestured for Claire to sit opposite him.

"I understand that was quite rude. It's just well, Malcolm was a good friend of mine, and he spoke fondly of a niece, but had not seen her in many years."

"I hadn't seen him since I was seventeen," Claire said. "It was only after his passing that I came back to town. I didn't mean to intrude, Casey it's just… the aged care facility mentioned your name. They said you were a close friend of his. I suppose I hoped you might help me understand more about the man he became. I hadn't seen him in years."

Claire decided to proceed gently rather than launch into talk of codes, letters, and hidden meanings. She didn't know him. He didn't know her.

Over the next thirty minutes, they talked about Malcolm, his interest in the church from a study point of view; its structures, rituals, and rhythm. Casey explained how he and Malcolm had, over the years, become good friends, often having friendly debates around Christianity, memory, and meaning. The conversation drifted to the town diner and its impeccable strawberry rhubarb pie, which caused Claire's stomach to rumble with distraction; a sudden realization that she hadn't eaten since yesterday.

Picking her moment, Claire leaned over toward Casey, her hand absently touching the wedding ring she wore on a chain.

"You said before that words were how you carried your meaning. The importance of a well-written liturgy. How a good priest can make people feel valued, like their presence matters.
Well... someone kept your words literally. I found a letter. Signed by you. In my uncle's house."

Casey frowned, confused then his expression shifted to one of relief. "He received that letter? I didn't know he had. I never got a reply. Toward the end... well, Malcolm's memory started to slip. We had started to figure certain things out about Ashridge Hollow. Maybe things we shouldn't have. Some of it I knew from before, but there were newer things Malcolm was uncovering.

But the dementia… it got to him before he could make sense of it all."

Claire studied him, his expression full of something that looked like grief. "It mattered to him, didn't it. What he was looking into? Help me honour that. Tell me what you know."

Casey broke down. First a whimper, then tears.

"I'm sorry. I… I'm a priest now. I've changed. Malcolm saw that. He became friends with who I was after. After I left the Order."

There it was again. *The Order*. Claire thought back to the decrypted journal entry and hesitated. She could tell him about it but didn't. Not yet.

She gently placed a hand on his.
"My uncle was a smart man, Casey. He won awards. Wrote research papers. I loved him deeply. He wasn't prone to wild theories unless it was about Walmart prices," she added with a half-smile. "If he trusted you, I'll honour that. So, help me understand. In the letter you said you'd found something but it didn't fit. What was it? What records?"

Casey drew in a breath. When he spoke again, it was slower, the tone of a man weighing every word.

"It wasn't always like this," he began. "When I was younger, I wasn't a priest. I was a businessman. A good one, too. I owned a car dealership in Albany and a small coffee franchise. I worked hard. Sure, I had some startup money from the old man, but I didn't waste it. Things were going great until the economy turned. Suddenly, people stopped buying local started going to Springfield. More options. Cheaper. And me? I didn't know what to do."

He sniffled lightly, pulling a handkerchief from his coat pocket.

"A business colleague told me about a group that helped people like me. Said it was simple just attend a few meetings, meet some nice people. And at first, it was fine. Business picked up. They helped me restructure some debts. Gave me a loan when I needed it. I thought it was just kindness.

But I didn't see what they wanted in return, not right away. Years passed, and I was still part of it. I couldn't walk away, not easily. They trusted me. Gave me responsibility. A title. Purpose. They felt like friends. Family, almost.

I saw glimpses of the darker side... but I kept my eyes shut. I told myself it wasn't my place. That I didn't know the whole picture. That maybe it wasn't as bad as it seemed. But deep down, I knew.

And one day call it a spiritual awakening if you like, I just couldn't do it anymore. I walked away. I thought I was done with it."

He paused, then looked at Claire with eyes that had stopped trying to pretend they were dry.

"But it's not the kind of thing you leave cleanly. Not something you quit with a resignation letter and a farewell cake. I only got out because I promised my silence. That's what they wanted. My silence. My distance. My disappearance. I gave it to them."

He inhaled through his nose, sharp and unsteady.

"And it still wasn't enough. They didn't threaten me, not directly. They didn't need to. They just reminded me what I had seen. What I'd been part of. And then they reminded me that I had a daughter. A life. A reputation that wouldn't survive daylight. So I left. I left everything. Started over. This collar isn't just faith, Claire, it's armour."

He exhaled, a long, worn breath that sounded like something he'd been holding in for decades.

"Malcolm was the only one from that time who still spoke to me like I mattered. Everyone else either vanished or got very good at forgetting. But your uncle… he kept digging. Even when it hurt."

They continued to talk in the church office.

Claire was just starting to relax, despite the weight of the conversation she felt no threat from Casey.

Casey had poured his story out like a man finally allowed to grieve. She'd watched his face crumple and smooth, the tension fall from his shoulders like dust from an old robe. He had offered her tea in a mismatched mug and even cracked a joke about Malcolm's taste in jazz.

The room had softened.

But as Claire reached to grab her coat from the chair, her eyes landed on a manila folder half-tucked beneath a stack of hymnals on Casey's desk.

Something about the way the corner peeked out; just a flash of stamped red text and a handwritten note in block capitals froze her. The moment stretched.

Casey noticed. He moved almost too casually, lifting a Bible and sliding the folder fully beneath it in one smooth motion. "Old donation records," he said lightly. "Messy filing system. I know. Malcolm would scold me."

Claire offered a polite nod. But her mind had already taken a snapshot.

She was almost sure the folder had said:
"INTERPRETER LIST: ARCHIVE COPY."

Leaving the church and walking toward her white sedan, Claire felt like she had more questions than answers.

They came at her like starbursts, quick and jarring:
Who were the Order?
What was in the folder Casey covered so quickly?
Had he ever truly left the group, or was that just something people told themselves?
Was it just a club for people who wanted to feel important?
If so, why the guilt in Casey's voice?
And why would her uncle who was always so rational treat it like a sociological experiment with no defined outcome?

She sank into the driver's seat and glanced at her phone. A message from Citra had come through: a photo of her grinning next to a scowling Eggroll, clearly offended by the ambush. Claire let herself smile. With the window up and the heater humming, she felt briefly protected just long enough to adjust her posture, slow her breathing, and gather her thoughts.

Apple and rhubarb, she mused aloud, starting the car and pulling out toward the diner.

Casey's Coffee was a town icon. It was not particularly elegant, but that alone made it perfect for Ashridge Hollow. Its low-key façade, flickering neon sign with half-lit letters, and weather-beaten boxy exterior gave it the look of a place time had passed over. The paint was white once, now flaked and tired, wooden slats curling from sun and snow. Only the deck looked new, recently rebuilt, bright and sturdy, like someone had tried to give the old place a facelift but ran out of money or care after the first attempt.

Inside, though, it was spotless. A long stainless steel counter ran the length of one wall, flanked by worn stools that looked more charming than rusty. The booths were classic red vinyl, and every table screamed *Americana* without the slightest hint of shame. It had been running since the 1950s, still owned by the same family. And they kept it like a shrine.

As a kid, Claire never thought much of it. But now, she saw its purpose. The worn-out look wasn't laziness. It was camouflage. It kept the tourists and day-trippers from bothering. Only locals knew the truth: step inside and you'd find warmth, pride, and the closest thing to tradition this town had left.

She was beginning to wonder just how many secrets Ashridge Hollow still held.

Settled in a booth near the centre, Claire finished her second-to-last bite of apple and rhubarb pie, phone resting nearby. A call came in with unfamiliar number, but the Ashridge area code caught her attention. She answered. Silence. Then a soft click as the line disconnected.

Can this day get any weirder? she thought.

"Hey Claire! Claire, is that you? Little Claire!"

She turned, adjusting her glasses, and saw him.

Jesse Calder.

Taller than she remembered, though it was hard to judge while seated. He loomed with an easy familiarity that brought back more than a few memories. He looked... good. The same, and not the same.

"I can't believe it's really you," he said, that grin spreading across his face. "I spotted you from across the diner. How long's it been? Fifteen, sixteen years?"

"Eighteen," she replied, smiling as she tucked a strand of hair behind her ear. "You always did struggle with math."

"And you always corrected me." He chuckled. "May I?"

She gestured to the seat across from her. "Of course. But don't let me eat any more pie, Jesse. I swear, I'll leave here three hundred pounds heavier."

"You know it's still the same recipe from when we were kids," he said, sitting down and flashing those infuriatingly perfect teeth.

"So, what are you doing these days? Let me guess you became the town vet or something?" she teased, knowing full well how much he used to loathe the farm chores his parents made him do.

"Well, see that new wooden deck out front?" he said, nodding toward the entrance. "Built it last week. I do carpentry now. Volunteer firefighting on the side but with winter coming, weekends are a bit quieter lately."

Claire, always the overthinker, clocked the phrase immediately. *Weekends are free.* Was that just a statement... or an invitation?

They talked for nearly an hour. Banter

about everything, and also about nothing at all. Against her better judgment, she had more pie. The waitress checked in just often enough to make it clear she was listening, as only small-town waitresses could. Half-service, half-intel-gathering. Claire didn't mind. It felt... charming. Familiar. Like she was stepping back into something she didn't realize she'd missed.

And Jesse? He was easy to talk to. Maybe the pie helped. But it was also something else; a kind of warmth, gentleness. He didn't bring up her parents, and didn't need to. They'd broken up only six months before the accident, not for any dramatic reason, just the natural decay of teenage fire. That hour together made it clear: he hadn't forgotten any of it.

Jesse's life felt grounded. No drama. No ex-spouses or custody battles. Just a pickup truck, a close-knit friend group, a volunteer shift here and there. He declined a call while they talked, didn't even glance to see who it was. That small gesture landed more than he knew.

As she got up to leave, he scribbled down his number.

Welcome back to Ashridge, she thought. Well… at least the day improved.

That night, Claire checked into the Ashridge Pines Motel; the town's finest by default. The rooms were a firm three-star experience: clean sheets, old heating units that rattled just enough to count as white noise, and lamps that worked if you wiggled the switch just right.

She wasn't sure what exactly had happened the night before at her uncle's place. A dream, break-in, or sleepwalking mystery; but she no longer felt comfortable there.

The motel reminded her of her New York apartment. One door. One window. One light switch to control everything.

Safe.

Comfortable, even.

But no Eggroll.

And for the first time in a while, she missed him more than she expected.

Claire stepped out of the bathroom, towel wrapped around her head like a makeshift crown, steam still clinging to the mirror behind her. She padded barefoot across the motel room's thin carpet, letting the warmth of the shower linger as long as it could. The heater hummed softly: old, rattling but reliable.

Dressed now in a loose jumper and leggings, she set her laptop on the small table near the window, cracked it open, and clicked to connect a video call.

The screen blinked.

Then Citra's face appeared: dimly lit, framed by the familiar chaos of her studio apartment. In the background, Eggroll was mid-pounce on what looked like a dangling sock.

"Hey!" Citra said, adjusting her glasses. "You look like you just emerged from a cave."

"I did," Claire said. "The Motel Ashridge spa experience: one small, suspiciously loud shower, zero pressure, but excellent existential reflection time."

Citra grinned. "I swear, every time you go somewhere rural, you level up in sarcasm."

From the side of the screen came a sudden, dramatic *Meow*.

Claire's face softened instantly. "Eggroll!"

Citra tilted her webcam just enough to reveal the cat, now parked firmly beside her keyboard, tail flicking like a metronome of discontent.

"He's been judging me all day," Citra said. "I think he misses the subway sounds."

"Does he miss me?"

"Hard to say. He might be planning a coup. He dragged a pair of my socks into his food bowl this morning."

Claire laughed, her shoulders relaxing. "Classic Eggroll. No act of rebellion is too petty."

Another meow. Louder. Claire leaned toward the screen.

"Tell him I miss him, and that no one makes me feel guilty for existing quite like he does."

"I'll translate it into passive-aggressive silence for him," Citra said, giving the cat a scratch behind the ears before turning her attention back. "So… tell me everything. How's it been?"

Claire hesitated, then let out a breath.

"Harder than I thought," she admitted. "Going back to the house… it was like stepping into someone's memory. His presence was everywhere. Like he'd just stepped out of the room for tea."

Citra nodded softly, listening.

"But it's not just emotional. I found a letter. Hidden in a drawer. From a man named Casey Weaver. He's a local priest now, but apparently, he and my uncle were… investigating something. It was cryptic, but it mentioned a group. Called 'The Order.'"

Citra sat up straighter. "Wait, what?"

"I know how it sounds," Claire said. "But the letter talked about dates not lining up, someone trying to bury records, and a place Malcolm would know how to find. There was even a hidden cipher in one of his journals. I cracked part of it with Ada. Names. Roles. People who'd been erased."

Citra blinked, then gave a low whistle. "Claire, that's not a letter. That's the opening scene of a conspiracy docuseries on Netflix."

"I know. And I met the priest Casey. He seemed genuine. Kind, even. But... something about the way he talked and the folder I saw him try to hide at the end of our visit. I don't know. It's not adding up yet."

"Did he mention this Order?"

"He did, but said it was something he walked away from. He called it a dark chapter of his life. That's all I've got so far."

Citra leaned back, folding her arms.

"It's exciting," she said. "But Claire... be careful. This isn't just family history. If there's a group like that, even if it's just old rich guys playing secret club, they won't appreciate someone poking around in their past. Especially not someone with a search engine for a brain."

Claire nodded. "I know. I'm being careful."

"Promise?"

"Promise."

Eggroll let out a long, guttural meow as if to second the warning.

Claire smiled. "Tell him I'll keep my claws sharp."

"I think he expects you to bring tuna back as tribute."

They both laughed, and for a moment, the tension eased; just two friends chatting across counties, connected by trust, humour, and the quiet weight of something neither of them could yet name.

After the call ended, Claire stood, glanced outside.

The street was still. A crow called once, then fell silent. Claire stared at her reflection for a beat longer than she meant to.

Then, quietly, she shut the lid of the laptop.

As the call came to an end, a data centre in Maryland hummed with quiet precision.

Somewhere in a server farm hidden beneath a nondescript government facility, packets of information were being sorted. Nothing unusual, just a stream of binary: ones, zeroes, metadata, cross-referenced tags. It happened millions of times a day. But this time, something clicked.

A match.

A video call from Ashridge Hollow had used a combination of flagged keywords.
The Order alone wouldn't have raised a signal. Nor would *Casey Weaver*, or even *Ashridge*; a sleepy town barely on any map that mattered.

But together?
The Order. Ashridge. Secret organisation. Casey Weaver.

That combination hit a threshold.

The conversation was flagged, mirrored, transcribed, and added to an encrypted queue for senior review. IP address. Device ID. Call duration. Transcribed dialogue. Flag weight: Medium-High.

Claire didn't know it yet.

She believed she was unravelling a forgotten mystery, a thread left by her uncle, a local priest, and a half-buried group once held together by loyalty and silence.

But elsewhere in a quiet room where fluorescent lights never turned off someone now considered *her* the anomaly.

A puzzle.

One that might need solving.

The weekend passed not in scenes but in moments that were stitched together like quiet thread.

Claire hadn't planned to spend more time with Jesse. But after their run-in at the diner, it felt natural. Familiar. A slow unspooling of whatever had once bound them. It was not dramatic, just... real.

They went walking just outside town, a trail Jesse knew by heart. She teased him for pretending it was a hike when it barely inclined, and he retaliated by pretending to get lost only to lead her straight to a ridge with a view of the entire valley, bathed in afternoon light. They sat there longer than either expected.

Later, they picked up takeaway from the same pizza place they used to sneak slices from in high school. He still ordered too much. She still picked the olives off. The town had changed. They hadn't.

That night, Claire didn't return to the motel.

She didn't need to say anything, and neither did he. In the morning, she woke with sunlight on her face, wrapped in a blanket that smelled faintly of cedar and old woodsmoke. Jesse was already in the kitchen, trying to figure out her tea preferences like it was a code worth cracking.

She smiled, watching him from the doorway. There was a comfort in it, not the kind that erased loneliness, but the kind that made it feel less permanent.

That afternoon, back at the motel, the comfort lingered like the faint scent of cedar still clinging to her cardigan. But Claire knew better than to let it settle. The coded list from the journal still waited.

She set her laptop on the desk, opened the window just enough to let in the breeze, and powered Ada back on.

Ready when you are, Ada said, the words blinking softly onto the screen as if in anticipation.

Ada's custom design from Citra had been built to filter through noise and surface the most probable result. According to Citra, it had a 99.7% success rate *but never rely on it completely,* she had warned. *Always verify.* Claire did verify. Sometimes. But mostly she'd just… gotten to know Ada. There was a kind of intuition between them now; not logic, not trust exactly, just familiarity. She could sense when to lean in, and when to question.

In the case of the names, Ada was already a step ahead. She'd run them through a tailored algorithm that linked name frequency, location, and context to isolate the most likely match; a necessity in a country of 347 million people, especially when 2.44 million of them apparently shared the surname Smith.

Claire typed the first name from the cipher: *Elijah Morran*. She hit enter.

Ada opened a tab to an obituary. Elijah had passed away in his sleep six months earlier.
A second tab showed he'd lived for years in Billings, Montana. Had a horse ranch. A quiet family life.

That would explain Northern Chapter, Claire mused. But it still didn't make sense how it would connect to a list of people in a town 2,000 miles away in Ashridge Hollow.

She typed in the second name: *Sarah Flynn. Former Initiate Southern Wing.*

Ada blinked to life, returning a flurry of results. Sarah Flynn was a wildly successful businesswoman based in Lafayette, Louisiana, founder of a cosmetics brand using locally sourced botanicals.

Claire studied the photos: high-end branding, polished press shots.
For someone selling natural beauty, Sarah's look was distinctly... laboratory-assisted. Lip filler, cheek work, the whole lot.

Still her eyes caught Claire's attention. Piercing, like they knew something.

Claire paused. Then clicked.

One click became five. Then fifteen. She dove into Sarah's social media, her corporate site, the press releases, the product line breakdowns, old interviews, even three years of corporate financials.

An hour passed.

She glanced at the time, rubbed her eyes, and refocused.

Okay. Table that for now. Doesn't scream Ashridge Hollow.

She typed: *Any record of her ever visiting New York State, beyond NYC?*

Ada responded instantly.

Two visits to New York City last year for board meetings. Both overnight stays. No time unaccounted for.

Claire raised an eyebrow. *That's specific. Where are you pulling that from?*

Private jet ADS-B tracking.
Departure logs confirm overnight stays only. Second trip departed directly to José Ignacio, Uruguay. Arrival confirmed at Capitan de Corbeta Carlos A. Curbelo International Airport.

Claire stared.

Nice for some, she typed. *Owning a jet and flying to a tropical paradise like it's just a casual Tuesday.*
Let's move on, Ada.

She entered the third name: *Nathaniel Cress. Keeper of Cycles.*
The title gave her pause. Something seasonal? Mechanical? It scratched at her brain, refused to settle.

Ada didn't respond right away.

The cursor blinked. Once. Twice. Then more.

Claire frowned. *Ada? Everything okay?*

Claire, everything is fine. The result is not tallying with expected status.

A browser tab opened. A news article from the *Santa Monica Mirror* described a boating accident near Catalina Island. A day-Sailer had struck Eagle Reef. Solo sailor. Fatal injuries. Wreckage recovered.

The name: Nathaniel Cress.

Another article revealed he'd been an insurance adjuster.

Claire stared at the screen. The title, *Keeper of Cycles,* suddenly felt colder.

Ok Ada, I see what you mean. Let's leave that Scooby Doo mystery to the lovers of the Catalina Wine Mixer and move on shall we, referencing one of her favourite comedies.

71

Ada blinked back with a cheeky smiling emoji.

Claire smirked.

The next in the list was Casey Weaver. Ada, already a step ahead, had skipped Casey for now as if sensing he wasn't the thread to pull further just yet.

Jonah Hale has two flagged references, Ada typed.
Two are in the Ashridge Hollow Historical Registry. Catalogue entries exist, but the source documents are offline with physical access only, likely at the town archives.

Claire sighed through her nose. *Figures.*

She typed again: *No social media, no articles, no business records, no online presence at all?*

Ada responded with a single word. *No.*

Claire frowned. *This one feels intentional.*

It is statistically unlikely for this level of unavailability to occur naturally.

You're saying someone hid them.

I'm saying someone didn't want them found.

Claire stared at the screen for a long moment. Then opened her bag and pulled out the journal. She traced the faded ink, the strange, rigid symbol etched near Jonah Hale's name with her thumb.

"All right," she said softly. "Let's go see what they tried to forget."

The Ashridge Hollow Archives building didn't pretend to be modern.

Dust lingered like it paid rent. Near the entrance, there was a sharp, unmistakable smell. Like a rodent had met an unfortunate fate beneath the shrubbery and been left to quietly decompose.

Claire signed the visitor ledger in a room that smelled of decaying paper and lemon cleaner. The clerk behind the desk was more focused on a balloon-popping mobile game than offering anything beyond a curt hello. Without a word, they pointed Claire toward the basement reference stacks.

She passed filing cabinets that hadn't been labelled in a decade. In towns like Ashridge Hollow, digitisation had passed them by. Larger cities received grants for that kind of work but not small municipalities like this. Claire almost ached to see it; as a professional archivist, she felt a natural instinct to start scanning and cataloguing on the spot.

Local bylaws. Rail surveys. Zoning applications. Everything quietly out of time. Some boxes were partly open, their contents disordered as if the last person to touch them hadn't bothered to put anything back properly.

At first, Claire searched for the references Ada had given her, transposed into the small notebook she always carried. But then she got sidetracked for nearly an hour, mesmerised by old flood maps, admiring the hand-drawn charts, the delicate inkwork before finally remembering to focus.

The first reference led her to a high school yearbook for Ashridge Hollow High. It was dated 1922, its yellowed pages fragile and worn. Carefully, Claire turned them one by one until she came to the senior class photo.
Third row. *Jonah Hale*. Stern. Not smiling, but that said more about photographic style at the time than any personal disposition.

This spoke to a deeper meaning in the names list: they weren't all current people: as if this group ran through time. Far back.

Slightly bemused by the age of the reference Ada had flagged, Claire checked the next note in her list. It led her to a slim manila folder labelled *Zoning Forms, 1928–1939*.

Inside were several documents: floodplain reports, well locations, a hand-drawn map of the old coal roads.

Then something in the corner of a 1934 form caught her eye.

A name, pencilled faintly in the margin. *Jonah Hale*. But that wasn't what made her pause.

On the same document was a symbol. Not a logo. A mark.

Angular. Bold. Simple.

A stark black symbol. Ordinary at first glance, like a monogram. It looked like a capital T flipped upside down, joined tightly to a reversed capital E. The edges were sharp, the angles clean. It had the rigid symmetry of something official, architectural, almost; but the longer she stared, the more unsettling it became. It didn't feel designed. It felt declared.

She turned the page. Her heart thudded once then again.

The next map, dated 1946, bore the same mark. Bottom right corner. Fainter, but still there. A prominent stamp of approval in red signed *Mayor Jonah Hale*.

Claire studied the date again. Jonah Hale had managed to go from being in High School to town mayor in 12 years. Mayor at age of 29, no small feat.

Claire looked around the room, half-expecting someone to be watching.

No one.

She slid the documents into a neat pile and checked them out under a "copy for study" permit.
It felt like a formality; Claire suspected she could have walked out with an original copy of the Gutenberg Bible and the clerk would've continued popping balloons, unbothered.

Outside, the town felt… brisker. Maybe it was just the season turning, but something had shifted. The symbol had been a threshold and Claire wasn't ready to slow down.

Glancing at her phone, she noticed a missed call from Jesse. Images of him making tea drifted back: the way he'd studied the boxes like a man trying to crack an ancient code of her preferences. It had been a couple of days since they'd spoken, but that seemed right. Jesse had a new contract to finish, and Claire valued her independence the way America values fireworks and founding documents.

She made a note to return the call that evening. But first, Ada was calling.

Claire returned to the motel just after five. The light was low, that rich amber tone that made even cheap carpet look warm. She tossed her bag onto the spare bed and sat heavily beside it, pulling out the folder she'd checked out from the archives.

The symbol, that damn symbol, still pulsed in her mind. Like it had followed her back.

She opened the folder and slipped the zoning form free. Held it to the window briefly, studying the lines again. It was so plain. So deliberate.

Claire took a photo with her phone. Two, actually; one close, one angled. Just in case.

She turned to her laptop, fired it up, and brought Ada back online.

You're quiet, Claire typed.
Waiting, Ada replied.

She attached the photo of the symbol and dragged it into the console.
Tell me everything you can.

For a moment, nothing. Just the cursor blinking. Then Ada began to stream results; not on the surface of the screen, but in the backend logs. Fast. Too fast.

Claire leaned forward. *What are you doing?*

Symbol scan matched.
Hidden in metadata across 13,984 public-facing websites.

Claire froze.
Come again?

Non-visible embeds found in image headers, HTML comments, XML side-trees, favicon files, and SSL certificate notes.

Ada began listing categories:

Four federal government contract directories

Major e-commerce sites, including auto sales platforms and real estate hubs

Fifteen regional power utility websites

231 privately hosted blogs

A discontinued fan page for a 1990s sitcom

Local tourism sites. A church bulletin.

Your university's archive access page.

Claire blinked. *No. No way.*

All results confirmed. Symbol not visually rendered embedded at data level. Dates of inclusion vary.

She stared at the console.

Why would a 1930s zoning mark show up in the code for a site selling used Toyotas?

Either a coincidence... or someone wants to leave fingerprints only machines can see.

Claire sat back. The hum of the air conditioning felt louder than it should. Somewhere down the hall, someone was laughing. A TV maybe, or real.

Thirteen thousand websites.

The number didn't feel absurd. It felt intentional.

Claire reached for her tea, then stopped, hand halfway to the cup.

Can you show me when the symbol first appeared in the system?

Ada blinked. Then:

Earliest embedded instance: October 7, 1996. Timestamp on an encrypted modem support page hosted from Reston, Virginia.

Claire read it twice.

Okay, she typed slowly, *so this goes deeper than archives and zoning forms.*

Claire stared at the screen, its glow now the only light in the room. The numbers still scrolled in the background like a silent chant. She rubbed her temples, unsure whether it was the scope or the implication that unsettled her more.

Too much, she typed, more to herself than to Ada.
I need you to narrow it down.

Parameters?

Local. Within 50 miles of Ashridge Hollow. Business listings only. Prioritize those with physical addresses still in operation.

Understood.

Claire pushed the chair back slightly, the legs creaking across the laminate floor. The motel room felt suddenly tighter.

Outside, the wind shifted.

The first sound of rain hit the motel roof like a whisper turning into a voice. Then came the heavier drops. It wasn't a storm yet, but the kind of rain that settled in, like it planned to stay a while.

A flash of white leaked through the edge of the thick motel curtains.

Headlights.

Claire turned, just enough to see the shadow of motion. A car was pulling in. She heard the tires hit a patch of wet gravel, followed by a soft skid as they corrected. The engine didn't rev. It simply stopped.

The headlights stayed on. Bright. Too bright.

Claire held her breath.

She didn't move, didn't twitch the curtain. Whoever it was had parked directly in front of her room. Not one over. Not two down. Her room.

Still the lights stayed on.

Ada blinked gently on the screen, unaware.

Claire's fingers hovered over the keyboard.

Ada, pause search. Someone just pulled in. Parking right outside. Lights still on.

She didn't know why she typed it. It was reflex, maybe. As if the machine could share the moment. Hold it with her.

Then the lights shut off.

Claire froze.

A car door opened. Then nothing for a moment. Then steps. Wet-sounding, careful steps. Approaching… then angling away. Toward another unit.

She released a long, silent breath. Let the tension melt just enough to let her move again.

She typed slowly.

Resume.

Ada responded without commentary, back to task, as if nothing had happened.

Eleven active business sites within 50 miles contain the symbol in metadata. Three in Ashridge Hollow proper. Would you like to see them in order of earliest instance or current visibility metrics?

Claire didn't answer right away. She stood, walked to the window, and peeled back a corner of the curtain just an inch.

The car was parked, its colour either black or dark grey. Hard to tell in the wet. No one visible.

She let the curtain fall and stepped back.

Visibility, she typed.
Let's start with who still wants to be seen.

Ada blinked once, then the screen shifted.
First result: *Ashridge Hollow Town Council.*

Claire clicked.

The page loaded slowly, as if reluctant. Typical. A half-broken banner image, a public meeting notice from four months ago, and links that hadn't been updated since someone's nephew interned in 2016. But there hidden in the site's source code, Ada highlighted it in faint yellow: *the symbol.* The inverted T joined with the reversed E.

She felt her throat tighten.

Next: Maggie's Place Diner.

Claire frowned. Maggie's? She and Jesse had eaten there only days ago. The website was barely a website; just a static image with operating hours and a menu PDF. But again, buried deep in the code, was the symbol.

Two additional council-affiliated pages contain references: archive index mirror and utilities ledger site.

Claire sat forward.

Show me.

The first led to a mirror of the local archives' online index, a backup of their old database. Not much there, but in the metadata of a file tagged *Legacy – Site Survey 1931*, the symbol returned.

The second page was stranger: a public utilities billing portal. But Ada had traced the symbol to a CSS template, tucked beneath layers of formatting logic, but there.

Who designed these sites?

Ada took three seconds.
Unknown. Domains registered via third-party services, site code likely based on reused internal templates. Pattern suggests long-standing institutional reuse, not external breach.

Still feels planted.

Or preserved.

Claire stared at those words longer than she meant to.

Then her phone buzzed.

Two missed calls. No voicemail. Unknown number.

She blinked.
The car.
Was that before or after the calls?

She checked the timestamps. About ten minutes ago. Right before the headlights had appeared.

Coincidence, she told herself. Just a late-night check-in.

But it didn't sit right.

She moved the laptop gently aside, letting the screen dim. Rain still tapped the windows, steadier now. More confident.

One more thing, Ada typed.
The man listed as registrar for the archival index mirror — one Everett Langford — is still active in the system. Last login: 11 days ago. Age: 72. Current residence listed as Ashridge Hollow.

Claire's mind snapped into focus.

Can you give me a location?

Affiliated with the archives building. No residential address listed.

Then tomorrow, she thought, she'd go back. Not just to dig. To talk.

To meet the man still watching over the town's forgotten knowledge. She stared at the rain for a moment longer, then closed the laptop.

The archive felt even quieter than before.

Claire paused at the front desk, but no clerk appeared. No balloon popping. Just the faint hum of fluorescent lights and the deeper silence beneath them.

She signed the visitor sheet without being asked. The pen was the same: chewed. The same lemon-cleaner tang clung to the air. But something felt... off. More off than usual. The door hadn't clicked behind her. The wind must've caught it wrong.

She headed past the same dusty cabinets, walking the narrow corridor with practiced steps. Her boots echoed slightly.

Ada's data still ran through her mind. The symbol. The connections. The names. And now this: a needling instinct that something here, something physical, had been left behind for her. Not sent. Not coded. Hidden.

She stopped at the "Community Events" cabinet. It was partly open. Not by much but just enough to break the clean line of closed drawers.
Claire tilted her head.

She pulled it open.

Nothing alarming. Parade rosters. Bake sale flyers.
Faded posters from town fairs and scout car washes.

Then

 one folder, unlabelled, manila, worn at the edges.

She slid it free.

Inside: were photocopied newspaper clippings.
Dozens.

Some she recognized. Names she hadn't thought of in
years. The girl who vanished the summer Claire turned
twelve. The mechanic whose boat "washed up empty"
in the river. A teenage boy found drowned in the
reservoir, ruled a late-night accident.

Every story had the same shape: Went missing. Local
search. Family upset. Authorities dismissive. Case
quietly closed.

But that wasn't the worst of it. In two of the older
photos, Claire spotted it.

In one: a silver brooch, worn by the woman found
face-down in a creek.
In another: barely visible graffiti behind the crushed
shell of a sedan wrapped around a tree.

The same symbol.
T flipped, joined to the reversed E.

Claire's stomach twisted. There was a realisation here that this order, their machinations, were much darker than Claire had wanted to consider. She closed the folder carefully, tucking it under her arm. She glanced around. Still no one.

No one except the man now standing at the end of the aisle, watching her with mild curiosity.

He was older. Seventy, maybe more. Pale sweater, grey pants, shoes too polished; the kind of shine that comes from habit, not vanity. A faded staff badge hung from a lanyard that might've once been blue.

"It didn't used to rain like this," he said softly, glancing toward the high windows.

Claire froze mid-step.

Something about him was off-kilter; not alarming, just… loosened. A little untethered. The way some old men talked to themselves in museums, except this one was looking directly at her.

"Everett Langford?" she asked.

He didn't nod. Just let a half-smile tug at one side of his mouth.

"I told them the archives breathe," he said. "Not metaphorically. Actually breathe. The dust isn't dust. It's memory."

Claire said nothing.

He looked past her; not at the shelves, not at anything visible. As if someone else stood just behind her shoulder.

"You hear them sometimes. Especially when it's quiet. I don't answer anymore. But I used to. That's probably when things started slipping."

His voice wasn't shaky. It was precise. Calm in the way engineers sound when describing plane crashes.

Then his eyes flicked back to her, briefly clearer.

"I remember you when you were young," he said. "You went to school with my daughter. She's gone now. Doesn't speak to me. Doesn't care to. But you be careful, Claire. Ashridge isn't what you think it is."

Claire's throat tightened. She gently tucked the manila folder deeper into her bag.

"I was hoping you could tell me about a document you last accessed"

"Eleven days ago," he said.

Claire's mouth paused mid-sentence.

"I know," Everett continued. "She told me you'd ask."

Claire blinked. *She?*

"Who?"

He tilted his head, like the question amused him. Then offered a different kind of answer.

"Not who," he said quietly. "When."

The air seemed to bend a little, as if something deeper had been spoken without being explained.

"I used to work for them, when I still had use. When I could code. Before my memory became... like a sponge."

He turned then, without urgency, and walked back into the filing cabinets. Each step was soft. Not the shuffle of age, but the kind of departure that didn't expect to be followed.

Claire stayed rooted to the floor.

Something about following him felt like it would offer only more questions. And questions, Claire already had plenty of.

The folder pressed against her ribs as she stood in the empty aisle, heartbeat slowing but not yet still.

She waited until she could no longer hear his steps. Then reached for her phone.

Two missed calls again. Unknown number. *Why didn't I hear it ring?* She stared at the screen.

Then looked back toward the aisle Everett had vanished into.

It was empty.

The rain had stopped, but the air still felt moved, unsettled in that way it sometimes is after a storm.

Stepping out of the archives and back onto the street as the last drops of rain ceased, Claire sat in the car for a moment, the manila folder still on the passenger seat. It felt heavier than it should; not just in weight, but in implication. Those names. The brooch. The clipped language of accidents and drownings.

She needed to speak to Casey.

Driving down to the church, Claire parked close and approached the door with purpose, the folder tucked under her arm. This time she didn't knock. She pushed the door open only to freeze as she was met by an unfamiliar face.

A young man with a buzzcut and a polished warmth turned from the altar, caught mid-preparation. His clerical collar was crisp, his smile practiced.
"Ah, you must be looking for Father Weaver," he said with a gentle cadence. "I'm afraid he's moved on."

"Moved on?" Claire asked, not quite hiding her suspicion.

"Reassigned, I believe. Diocesan transfer. I've only been here a day or two myself. But I'm happy to help if I can."

Claire offered a thank-you, but it landed flat. The sanctuary was spotless, no trace of Casey anywhere. No clutter, no handwritten notes, no coffee mug tucked behind the organ. Just a clean-swept space and a faint trace of cedarwood polish.

The young priest's eyes drifted to the folder in her hands. Claire instinctively clutched it tighter.

"Thanks that's okay. I should be going," she said quickly, already turning toward the exit.

Back in the car, Claire sat for a long moment with her hands on the wheel. That made two times in one week she'd left a church feeling more unsettled than she entered.

No wonder I'm not religious, she muttered.

She pulled out onto the road, trying to let the tension slip away, only to see the flashing red-and-blue lights appear in her rearview mirror.

The flashing red-and-blues appeared in her rearview mirror just as Claire was turning back onto the main road toward the motel.

She sighed, pulling over without protest.

A light drizzle misted the windshield as the silhouette of the officer approached. He had wide shoulders, impeccably ironed uniform, flashlight already drawn, not even trying to shield it from her eyes.

She rolled the window down halfway.

"Everything alright, officer?" she asked, keeping her voice measured.

No reply at first. Just the flashlight sweeping the interior. Her bag. The rental paperwork on the passenger seat. The empty peppermint tea cup in the console.

"Step out, please."

Claire blinked. "Is there a reason"

"Routine inspection."

She complied. The asphalt was damp beneath her boots. The cold seeped in through her cardigan.

The officer's badge read "BANNERMAN".He circled the car slowly, crouching once, then again. He took out a small metal ruler. Measured the tread depth on both front tires. Checked her license plate. Checked the VIN through the windshield. Even opened the rear door unprompted.

Claire stood still, arms crossed, a small trickle of drizzle falling again.

He said nothing for five more minutes. Just scribbled.

Her phone buzzed. She answered without even glancing at the screen.

"Citra," she said quietly, turning slightly away. "I'm pulled over by the side of a road for having the wrong kind of tyre wear in a town with no Uber. How's your night?"

A pause. Then Citra's voice, filtered and fuzzy: "What?"

"It's been a day. First, a car pulls up and just stares at my motel room last night. Then I find a missing persons folder basically gift-wrapped in a fake archive drawer. And now, Officer Bannerman here is giving my rental sedan the TSA treatment."

She glanced back. He was still writing. Slowly. Like the ink needed coaxing.

"You okay?"

"Yeah. Just…" Claire lowered her voice. "It feels like someone's checking how much I'm willing to tolerate."

Citra was silent for a moment. Then: "Call me after. And text me the policeman's id just to be safe."

Claire nodded instinctively. "Will do."

Officer Bannerman returned at last, three folded pink slips in hand.

"Tread under regulation," he said flatly. "Rear wiper blade split. Side mirror casing loose."

"It's a 2023 Corolla," Claire said, half-smiling. "Do they all come out of the factory broken?"

The officer didn't react.

He handed over three citations and turned without a word.

Claire got back in, started the engine, and pulled away slowly. In the rear-view mirror, the cruiser didn't move. It just sat there headlights dimmed, its occupant still watching. Rigid. Expressionless. Like a checkpoint that had always been there, waiting.

Back at the motel, she barely let the door swing shut before reaching for her bag. She unzipped it and pulled out the manila folder, newspaper clippings spilling across the bed in faded, brittle waves.

One in particular caught her eye: a short article about a local woman found face-down in a creek. Early thirties. Cause of death listed as a sudden heart attack leading to pulmonary oedema. But what drew Claire's attention was the accompanying photo: a silver brooch still pinned to the woman's jacket. The same symbol Claire now knew was connected to the Order.

The article felt... off. The language was unusually clinical; the kind of medical specificity that didn't belong in a local news write-up. Not unless it was trying to sound official. Trying to bury the strangeness beneath authoritative terminology.

A message, Claire thought. A warning. Maybe not to the public, but to a specific someone. *You cross us, your heart might stop too.*

A car pulled into the lot outside; tires slick against the rain-dark pavement. Claire paused, breath caught. Her nerves were frayed, stretched tight from everything today. Every sound now felt like a signal. A coded knock. Fight or flight.

She focused back in, typed the woman's name into Ada with the date and location of the article.

A moment passed. Then:

This name has been erased from multiple records. That usually indicates deliberate obfuscation. Claire, the data was there. The metadata indicates it. But the data itself is gone.

Claire frowned.
Are we talking a few sites or many? What kind of data, and from where?

Erased from local news archives, government records, and obituary aggregators. A reference still exists on a relative's Facebook feed, but the original profile it linked to has been deleted.

Claire leaned back. This was no longer just strange, it was systemic.

She stared at the bed, then began jotting two columns into her notebook: *Reasons to Stay* and *Reasons to Leave.*

Stay:

- Finish estate paperwork.

- See it through, for Malcolm.

- Something is here. Too much to ignore.

Go:

- The folder.

- The priest switch.

- The cop.

- The car.

Her pen hovered.

She knew herself. If she stayed, she'd dig. And if she dug, she wouldn't stop.

"Stuff it," she muttered.

She would stay, but she'd be smart about it. She picked up her phone and opened a message to Citra.

Still in Ashridge. Weird day. Tell you tomorrow. Will check in daily from now. Just in case.

She hit send.

Then she looked back at the symbol. The silver brooch. The missing name.

This wasn't just a trail anymore. It was a pattern and she was already in it.

The next morning arrived without ceremony.

No nightmares. No revelations.

Just light pressing through the motel curtains and the hum of tires on wet asphalt outside. Claire didn't linger. She dressed simply and slid the folder back into her bag, its contents still rattling around in her mind like stones in a jar. She wasn't ready to dig again, not yet.

Instead, she texted Jesse. *Breakfast?*

He replied within seconds. *Already at the booth. Coffee's hot. Just missing company.*

It was still early when she stepped back into the diner. The same bell above the door jingled. Same floor tiles with that one cracked corner near the register. For a moment, it felt like it could've been ten years ago. nothing changing except the faces behind the counter. Jesse looked up and grinned, motioning her over with a raised coffee mug.

He wore that same plaid shirt from yesterday, or one just like it. Some people didn't need variety to feel grounded. "Morning," Claire said as she slid into the booth opposite him. "Morning," he said, passing her the sugar like muscle memory. "You look… less haunted than yesterday."

She laughed.
"That's just good lighting."

They talked casually at first; weather, old teachers, the firehouse. Claire listened more than she spoke, but found herself nodding along with familiarity she hadn't expected to resurface.

Jesse had a grounding effect. A feeling of being a safe harbour in the storm of her thoughts. He wasn't trying to impress her. He wasn't asking questions. Just being there.

After a while, Jesse's phone buzzed. "Gotta take this. Back in a sec."

He stood, stepping outside, leaving Claire alone with the gentle clink of cutlery and low diner chatter. A waitress approached. She was older than Claire, but familiar. Somewhere in the blur of high school memories, Claire placed her: a few years above, always quiet, used to run cross-country.

The woman refilled her mug, then lingered just a second longer than needed.
"You seem like a good person, Claire," she said, her voice low. "Just… be careful who you trust."
Claire blinked. "Sorry?"
The woman's eyes didn't quite meet hers. She glanced

toward the window, where Jesse stood outside, back turned, on the phone.

"People around here aren't always who they once were," she continued.

"People change." And just like that, she moved on. Back behind the counter. As if she'd never said a word.

Claire sat perfectly still for a beat. The warmth of the coffee mug felt suddenly too warm. She smiled politely as the waitress passed by again, a reflex, nothing more; then looked back out the window. Jesse was still talking, animated, smiling at whoever was on the line. He turned, caught her eye and gave a smile.

Just a guy from town. A familiar face. Still, something shifted.

Claire finished breakfast with Jesse, deciding to leave at the same time he departed for work. She didn't want to risk another solo encounter with the waitress.

Driving her sedan which, by all accounts of the local police, probably broke several road safety laws, Claire decided to head to Main Street for a little retail therapy. Never much of a shopper, she made an exception today. Something about immersing herself in Ashridge Hollow felt right. Grounding.

To her surprise, most of the shops were still open. Unlike many small towns across regional New York, Ashridge had somehow managed to survive the convenience of doorstep deliveries and the gig economy. Here, people didn't just support local businesses, they seemed to prefer them over cheaper, faster alternatives. It was another small oddity Claire's archivist mind filed away under *strange but notable*.

The first store she stepped into was a quaint gift shop. It was the kind that lived off potpourri, candles, and cards with watercolour flowers and vaguely inspirational quotes. She gently twirled one of the display stands, smiling at the woman behind the counter, who was busy tying a bow on a small box.

"Hey, I'm Claire. I grew up here. Lovely store. Those little gift bags near the door are adorable," she said genuinely.

The woman looked up and beamed. "Oh hey, Claire! Welcome back, then! Did you grow up in Ashridge? Tell me your last name. I used to be the receptionist at the high school. I'll bet I know it!"

Claire hesitated for a moment. "Halstead."

The woman's expression shifted, her rosy cheer draining into something softer, almost grey. "Oh... I'm so sorry, Claire. Truly. How are you after all these years?"

"I'm doing okay, trust me," Claire said, offering a half-smile. Still, the name stirred something in her chest. It was not grief exactly, but a heaviness that hadn't quite lifted. "I just came back to sort a few things for my uncle. Malcolm Halstead. Did you know him?"

The woman's face brightened. "Oh, Malcolm! He was a laugh," she chuckled, her voice lifting again. "Always with those notebooks. Always interested in everyone's business. A curious one, in a good way, mostly. But toward the end, when his memory started going... well, he could get a bit much."

Claire kept her tone light, but leaned in. "What do you mean? It's okay, Betty, you can tell me. I know about

103

the dementia. Honestly, I'm trying to understand more about him after all this time away."

"Thank you, dear. I didn't want to speak out of turn. It's not very Ashridge of me, is it?" Betty leaned in now too, shifting from shopkeeper to old neighbour, lowering her voice the way only small-town locals do when something juicy is about to be shared. "Malcolm, toward the end… well, he started saying strange things. Going into shops. Asking questions."

Claire stayed quiet.

"He asked James at the butcher's why he was still open," Betty whispered. "Told him he'd run the numbers and there was no way the place was profitable. James kicked him out. But Malcolm kept coming back and pestering him. The police had to speak with him in the end."

Betty shook her head, the fondness returning despite her story. "But he didn't stop, not really. Just… shifted. He'd sit on that bench across the street, watching people. Taking notes. Sometimes scowling."

Claire followed her gesture to the bench. It sat empty now, across from the shop window, catching morning light like it had nothing to hide.

She didn't speak, but in her mind, she saw it clearly: Malcolm, pen in hand, eyes narrowed. Not just losing his grip on reality but trying, even then, to pull a thread that no one else could see.

Trying to make sense of something.

The bench lingered in her mind even as she walked further down the street. But something about the mention of James, the butcher, stayed with her. Malcolm had gone there often enough to be spoken to by police. That wasn't just dementia. That was persistence.

The bell above the butcher's shop door gave a hearty clang as she stepped in. The place smelled of smoked meats and floor bleach, too clean to be old, too lived-in to be new. A few cured sausages hung above a display of tightly wrapped cuts. Behind the counter stood a broad man in his early sixties with a fading red apron and the kind of arms that made it clear he still did the lifting himself.

"Morning," he said, not quite looking up as he adjusted a tray. "Help you with something?"

Claire offered a polite smile. "I'm actually not here for steak, sorry. Just had a quick question."

He looked up, wary now. "You with the council?"

That caught her off-guard. "No. I'm just... Malcolm Halstead's niece."

He paused. The name landed. Slowly, he set down his tray.

"Right," he said. "Malcolm."

Claire nodded. "I was told he used to come in here. Toward the end."

James leaned his elbows on the counter, exhaling through his nose. "That he did."

"Was he okay? I mean, people said he got a bit... eccentric."

James scratched his jaw, hesitating. "He was harmless."

"But persistent?" Claire tilted her head, gently.

A longer pause.

"Listen, I liked Malcolm. I did. But he got ideas. Thought everyone was hiding something. Came in here with these little notebooks, started asking about deliveries, my margins, who came in and when. I told him to piss off, politely, at first. But he wouldn't let it go."

Claire kept her expression neutral. "Why do you think he picked your shop?"

James's eyes flicked toward the back room too fast. "No idea. Just one of his fixations, I guess."

But something in the shift of his tone gave her pause. Claire followed that instinct.

"Did he ever find anything?" she asked, voice soft.

James stiffened slightly. His jaw tightened.

"Look," he said after a moment. "It's sad what happened to him. But Malcolm didn't always know what he was talking about. Dementia's cruel like that. Makes you see patterns where there's just life happening."

He started cleaning the counter, a signal.

"Anyway, I gotta shut early today. Inventory."

Claire blinked. "It's not even noon."

"Yeah. Still. Things to do."

She offered a polite nod. "Of course. Thanks for your time."

As she turned to leave, she caught the faintest twitch in his eye. Regret, maybe. Or worry that he'd said too much.

Back on the street, Claire walked slowly, hands in her jacket pockets.

She hadn't come here to investigate. But the story kept pressing back.

Claire pulled out of the angled parking bay in front of the florist, a small paper bag of peppermint bark riding shotgun. The early afternoon sun had burned through the morning drizzle, leaving Main Street washed and glistening, the kind of clean that made even memory feel newer.

She wasn't thinking about anything in particular. Not the folder. Not Ada. Just the gentle motion of the day until she caught it in the mirror.

A dark sedan. Not black, not grey; that indistinct in-between shade that looked like both. A car she'd seen before. Maybe at the motel? Or somewhere else?

She told herself it didn't matter. Just a coincidence.

But when she took a left, it took a left.

When she slowed to glance at a storefront, it slowed too.

Claire's fingers tapped the wheel lightly. A flutter of doubt, nothing more. Still, she decided to test it.

She signalled right, changed lanes early, took the long way around toward the back end of the town square, past the old post office, looping around the tiny municipal park.

The car followed.

No hesitation. No other traffic between them. Just the same steady presence two car lengths back.

Claire's pulse nudged higher.

She circled the block again, this time deliberately. Past the same bakery, the same teenager smoking by the laundromat, the same woman pushing a pram.

The sedan mirrored her again.

She exhaled sharply through her nose, jaw tight. One more time.

Third loop.

Halfway around, the sedan suddenly turned left, disappearing behind a row of townhouses.

Claire didn't follow. Didn't stop. Just kept driving, heart hammering a little harder now, the small paper bag rustling beside her with each subtle turn of the wheel.

By the time she reached the edge of the motel parking lot, the hum of suspicion had settled into something else; something colder.

And for the first time in years, Claire double-checked that her room door latched properly behind her.

With the door locked and latched, Claire made tea with the mechanical grace of someone moving through a checklist. She sat on the edge of the bed, phone in hand, and tapped in Citra's number. The line clicked faintly before ringing. Maybe just the signal. Still, it made her pause.

They spoke briefly. Claire didn't give everything away. Just enough: the news articles from the day before, the odd vibe in town, and the unsettling detail that she'd been followed. Citra told her to stay sharp. To be careful. Claire promised she would.

After the call, she opened her laptop.

Ada, what a day, she typed.

Claire, are you ok?
Your GPS pattern today indicates you circled the same block several times before returning to the motel. Were you concerned someone was following you?

Yeah. Just… note it.

Noted. You're not alone in this.

Claire exhaled, softened. It was strange; Ada was just code, just text on a screen. But right now, she felt like company. Not the same as human company. Maybe not even close. But real enough.

As the light outside dimmed and the motel room settled into evening quiet, Claire sank deeper into research. She and Ada worked in tandem. Cross-referencing documents, scanning archives, hopping between browser tabs and half-written notes. It wasn't methodical, but it was obsessive. A scatterplot of curiosity pulling her forward.

Her thoughts drifted back to earlier that day.

Ada, can you cross-check James W. Butcher Shop against local council documents, social media presences, any media articles?

110

Ada blinked then browser tabs bloomed like petals.

A standard Facebook business page. A local news piece: James donating meat at cost price to the retirement facility. A staged photo of him handing over trays of sausages, solemn expression, pressed shirt.

Council documents showed nothing unusual. Routine health inspections. A squeaky-clean record.

Ada, you're holding out on me. What is it?

Ada replied with a single winking emoji. Then another tab opened: a live feed. Council-run. A streaming camera from the park near Main Street, ostensibly there to monitor the nesting activity of local Barred Owls. Split screen: one zoomed tight on a hollow tree, the other a wide shot across the edge of town.

Claire leaned in. Her eyes caught it immediately.

The butcher shop. Barely in frame. But lit.

It was 8:03 p.m. The town was quiet, shops long since closed. Claire knew the rhythm of Ashridge Hollow well enough to know no one ran late-night deliveries here. Not without a reason.

She stared for a moment. Then quietly closed the laptop.

Reached for her keys.

One boot half-on, she was already out the door.

Claire didn't park directly in front of the butcher's. That would've been reckless; and besides, she had a hunch she wouldn't need to be close to see something strange.

She looped around the block first, then eased the car into a side street that curved gently behind the row of shops. From there, she had a partial line of sight to the back of the butcher shop through a gap between buildings. The street was dark with only one working streetlight humming weakly, its glow swallowed by the evening mist.

She killed the engine and let the silence settle. The kind of small-town silence that only exists when the shops close, the kids are indoors, and the main highway cuts around the town rather than through it bypassing the heart entirely.

Ashridge Hollow was quiet by design. Tonight, that quiet felt loaded.

The lights inside the butcher shop were still on.

A van sat backed into the alley, its rear doors yawning open. The engine was running with low, steady, a soft mechanical heartbeat in the stillness.

Claire sank lower in her seat.

From her angle, she could just make out the movement: two men, one older and built like a retired linebacker, the other wiry, almost twitchy. Both wore dark clothing. They weren't in butcher whites, and they weren't loading meat.

Each of them hauled out a large black rucksack, one in each arm, slow and heavy like they were carrying bricks. Or something worse.

Claire didn't move. She didn't even breathe for a few seconds.

She reached for her phone, turned off the flash and sound, and snapped two quick photos through the windshield. Then, heart thudding, she recorded a short clip. It was just enough to catch the second man dragging the last bag across the concrete and hoisting it into the back of the van.

The whole thing took less than five minutes.

The van's doors shut. No voices. No idle chat. Just the faint thunk of metal on metal, and the soft squeal of tires as the van reversed, then drove off without headlights for the first hundred meters.

Claire stayed parked for another minute, the weight of what she'd seen settling in. She didn't know what was in those bags and realistically, she might never know. But it sure as hell wasn't pork chops.

She considered the police. A rational person might've gone to them.

But she thought about the cop from two days ago. The way he'd stared at her like she didn't belong. The excessive tickets. The silence. The unspoken warning.

No. She wasn't going to the police.

Not yet.

She'd keep the photos, back them up, and let Ada cross-check every detail come morning.

But for now, she started the engine and drove back to the motel, quiet, headlights dimmed. Half hoping, half dreading that someone might be watching her too.

In the room Claire dimmed the lights and plugged her phone into the laptop. The footage transferred cleanly. It was blurry in parts, but clear enough to make out the figures, the bags, and the van's open rear.

She saved everything twice. Once to her desktop. Once to an encrypted drive she used for archival redundancy. A third copy she uploaded into Ada's secure storage partition.

Keep these safe, she typed.

Stored. Shall I begin object tagging and metadata extraction?

Do it.

A low hum of processing kicked in as Ada parsed the video frames. One of the men's faces was never visible, the other only briefly a grainy profile. Still, Ada worked frame-by-frame, isolating silhouettes, movement signatures, light discrepancies.

Claire took stills and printed them, her shaky hands feeding paper into her compact printer. She laid the photos out on the bed like puzzle pieces. The van was in almost every frame, angled just enough to obscure the plate.

Ada, anything on the vehicle?

Searching. Grey utility van. Rear-hinged doors. Appears to be a Ford E-Series, model range 2005–2009.

Can you cross-check against local registry data? Parking fines, property records, council footage?

Limited access to government databases. But… triangulating public footage tags and traffic images from the last 30 days in Ashridge Hollow.

Claire leaned back, her breath slow and shallow. The printer's last page spit out with a blurred shot of the second man mid-lift, the bag bending awkwardly under its own weight.

I found two partial matches. One van parked outside the grain co-op last Thursday. Another outside the maintenance entrance to the town library. Same model, same dent above the rear wheel.

Can you link them to a name?

No license plate confirmed. But there is a pattern forming.

Claire stared at the screen. Two sites. Both places with public blind spots. Both places she'd passed recently without noticing anything.

She reached for the photo of the van's shadowed grille and pinned it to the motel room's corkboard, just above the ones of the men. Her fingers hovered there for a moment; not touching, just hovering, then dropped to her side.

We're in it now, huh?

We are.

Claire didn't sleep much.

She'd dozed in half-hour pockets, waking to replay fragments of the video in her mind. By sunrise, the motel felt like a sealed capsule. It felt dim, airless, humming with unsaid things. She brewed a bitter coffee, left it untouched, and stared at her phone.

One message. Jesse.

Morning. If you're up for it, I'll be at home all day. I'm finishing a shelving job for the station. No pressure. But... you seemed off yesterday.

No pressure. But he noticed. And he was offering space, not answers, not interference.

Claire sat on the edge of the bed, thumb hovering over her screen. Then she typed, paused, deleted. Typed again.

I've got something I might want to talk about. You still at the house later this morning?

He replied almost instantly.

Of course. Come by any time.

She didn't overthink it. Just dressed, packed her notes, and drove.

Jesses' place was a low-built, cedar-sided home near the fire station, tucked beside a grove of tall pines. The yard was neat but not manicured; like someone who cared, just not obsessively. A worn basketball sat in the grass near the porch steps, and Claire could hear the rhythmic buzz of a table saw inside.

He opened the door before she knocked, wiping his hands on a rag.

"You look like you haven't slept," he said, voice easy.

"I haven't. That obvious?"

He smiled gently and stepped aside. "Come in. Coffee's probably better than motel sludge."

Claire followed him into a warm, open-plan kitchen with wide counters and the smell of sawdust faint beneath fresh toast. A half-assembled pine bookcase leaned against one wall, clamps still in place.

She settled at the table while he poured coffee into two mismatched mugs. He didn't push. Just sat down across from her, elbow on the table, watching without pressure.

Claire tapped her fingers against the ceramic. "I found something. In my grandfather's things. A journal entry. Weird. And a letter, from a priest."

Jesse tilted his head slightly. "A priest?"

"Yeah. Addressed to Malcolm. Dated just a couple of months before he went into the aged care facility. It was vague, but... it mentioned something. A shared burden."

She took a sip, then pulled a folded photocopy from her bag. It was the journal entry scanned and printed, with faint ink and odd symbols that had mystified her at first. Symbols appeared in the margins: a triangle, a half-sun, an unfinished date. Beneath them, Claire had scribbled her own notes, short, clipped, marked in red pen.

"I decrypted it," she said, laying it between them. "It was a cipher. He was hiding something. Not from himself but from whoever might read it after."

Claire flipped to the next page, revealing the deciphered text beside the original symbols, line by line.

Jesse leaned in and traced a line with his finger. "'Some stayed loyal. Some stayed silent.' Umm... okay."

"It's a reference to the names," Claire said. "My uncle Malcolm clearly felt burdened by what he knew. But he also knew time was running out with his own mind."

Jesse scanned the names slowly, eyes narrowing slightly when he reached one near the top.

"Casey Weaver," he said. "The priest?"

Claire nodded.

"Huh. Always thought he was a little too jovial for his own good," Jesse muttered. "Didn't recognize any of the other names, though."

But as he spoke, Claire noticed his finger hover under one entry, *Jonah Hale*. He didn't say anything. Just let his fingertip rest there a moment too long before moving on.

Claire opened her mouth, then stopped herself. Don't be ridiculous, she thought. You've just started trusting him. Don't ruin it with shadows.

Jesse looked up again. "You worked all that code transcription out on your own?"

"Mostly. Ada helped."

Jesse blinked. "Ada?"

Claire smiled. It was the first real smile in hours. "She's not a person. Ada's my AI assistant. Runs on my laptop. A friend built her for me back when I was still at Fordham."

Jesse leaned back slightly, like he was reevaluating the last five minutes of conversation. "Okay. That makes a lot more sense."

"She's just good at pattern recognition. Old texts, blurry handwriting, aligning dates. It's like having a second pair of eyes, one that doesn't sleep and doesn't get distracted."

Jesse nodded slowly, still eyeing the page. "Remind me not to play chess against you two."

Claire chuckled. "You'd lose."

There was a pause. Not awkward, just quiet. The kind that settled into the room like morning light. Then Jesse tapped the edge of the journal page again.

"So, what's the next step?"

Claire exhaled. "Keep digging."

"Well, I'm here and not too bad with a shovel," Jesse said, gently placing a hand on her shoulder.

That evening Claire sat cross-legged on the motel bed, the journal open again, though she wasn't reading. Her laptop screen cast a pale glow across the darkened room. Ada's window blinked once.

There may be one more path to consider tonight.

Claire leaned forward. *Who?*

Sarah Flynn. Former Initiate. Southern Wing. Lafayette, Louisiana. I found an active social presence. Personal Instagram account. Verified. High response rate to direct messages. Status: reachable.

Claire hesitated then opened the app. The account was easy to find. Lavish photos. Sunsets on rooftops. A cosmetics brand she vaguely recognized from airport shelves. It all looked perfectly curated, just like someone trying not to remember anything.

Claire tapped *Message.*

Hello. This is Claire. I'm looking into something and wanted to ask for your help. It's about "TE."

For a moment, nothing. Then the screen lit up.

Can you talk now?

Claire responded *Here's my number if you're willing to talk.*

A moment later, her phone buzzed. Unknown number. Claire answered on instinct.

A woman's voice came through. The voice was smooth, controlled, with a soft Southern undertone, like a news anchor trying not to let her real mood show.

"I can't stay on the line long," Sarah said. "But you need to stop whatever you're doing."

Claire sat up straighter. "I just want answers. My uncle Malcolm Halstead, well he passed away. I'm trying to finish what he started."

Sarah exhaled sharply through the receiver. "You think this is some noble mission?"

"I think there's something underneath all of this, and you were part of it."

There was silence. Then Sarah's voice again lighter this time, almost amused.

"Oh, Claire. It's not what you think. It's not some dark conspiracy. It's a gentleman's club with too much ceremony and too much money. I joined for the networking."

Claire narrowed her eyes. "The Southern Wing. What was it?"

"Social dinners. Insider deals. Everyone pretending they were smarter than everyone else." Her voice dipped lower. "But you want to hear the truth? The world runs on access. Power. Favors. You think any of your fancy institutions are immune to that?"

Claire didn't respond.

Sarah continued, voice hardening. "You get ahead by knowing the right people. That's all the Order ever was. A shortcut. And yes, sometimes that means doing things that aren't exactly pleasant. But they get results."

Claire's grip on the phone tightened. "Tell me what the Order *does*."

A beat of silence. Then a low laugh, not unkind, but bone-cold.

"You're still asking the wrong question."

"What's the right one, then?"

But Sarah didn't answer.

The call ended.

Claire stared at the screen for several seconds before lowering the phone. The room was quiet again motel air thick and still. Ada's cursor blinked softly on the laptop screen, waiting.

Claire didn't type. She just sat there, the weight of the conversation sinking into her bones.

She stood, walked over to the single window in the motel room, and pulled the curtain halfway open. Hands on her hips, she stared into the night. It was still the kind of stillness you only find in small towns. To the left, three lights shone from other motel rooms. One had the curtain drawn open, a baseball game flickering across a mounted TV. In the lot outside, three vehicles were parked: a RAM, a Ford F-Series pickup, and a small red sedan with its side window cracked and garbage bags taped over it, a temporary fix until the owner could afford better. The half-lit neon sign outside buzzed faintly, its reflection trembling on the pavement like it was protesting the power it drew. Further down, two teenagers rode past on bicycles, undeterred by the dark. *Nothing says small-town America quite like kids out riding late*, Claire thought.

Her mind drifted back to *The Order*. To their reach, their age. Sarah had both dismissed them and hinted at their strength in the same breath.

Even in middle America, where churches still filled on Sundays and old diners proudly survived, there was something darker under the surface.

Something waiting to be peeled back.

This wasn't some gentleman's club passing cigars and whispers. Claire had seen too much for that now.

The woman in the creek, the brooch.
The graffiti hidden behind the crash-site photo.
The way Casey spoke in careful riddles before disappearing.
Her uncle's encrypted journal entry.
The local cop's approach to her.
The butcher who looked a little too nervous, and his mysterious late night pickup.

Each piece on its own could be explained away.
Together, they formed a pattern.

The Order didn't operate in daylight, it never had.

And something she'd said to Sarah now echoed back with new clarity.
This wasn't just about her anymore. Sure, there was a mystery.
But it was also about Malcolm.

About making up for all the years she wasn't around. About finishing something he started.

Claire drifted into sleep without meaning to head still tilted against the motel headboard, laptop half-closed on the bedside table. Outside, a soft breeze tugged at the neon sign, and the distant hum of a truck came and went.

In her dream, the light was strange. Mute and golden, like early morning sun filtered through gauze. She stood in a house that felt familiar, though nothing matched the real layout of her uncle's home. The walls curved slightly inward, as if bowed by age or memory.

And there he was. Malcolm.

Younger than she remembered, his hair darker, his frame straighter. He stood in the kitchen, but it wasn't the kitchen from her childhood. This one had tall, narrow windows, and light poured through in long strips. He wasn't facing her. Just standing at the counter, his hands busy with something small.

Claire opened her mouth to speak, but no sound came.

He turned slowly, and in his palm, resting delicately like something sacred, was a brooch. The same one from the photo in the archive. Oval-shaped. Dark centre. Ornate edges, almost vine-like.

Malcolm looked at her, eyes gentle but tired. His lips moved. Once. Then again. But the words were muffled, as though coming from behind thick glass. Claire took a step forward, but the floor beneath her gave slightly, like she was standing on a damp book or something soft.

The brooch slipped from his hand.

She reached out too late.

It fell, landing with a sound like a bell in water.

Malcolm looked down at it, then up at her. His mouth opened again, and this time she almost heard it.

"Not what they said it was."

Claire blinked.

The dream fractured like a spiderweb hit by a stone. She awoke with a sharp inhale, heart pounding in her chest, fingers curled in the motel bedsheets. The bedside lamp flickered once before holding steady.

The room was still.

Claire sat up and touched the ring around her neck, grounding herself.

The next day at his house, Claire had commandeered the corner table of Jesse's small sunroom, a space just big enough for two chairs, a potted fern, and a view of the backyard where soft rain tapped the leaves. Her laptop was open, Ada running quietly in the background.

Jesse stood beside her, arms folded, peering at the screen.

"So… Nathaniel Cress," Claire said. "Title was *Keeper of Cycles*. Whatever that means."

Jesse smirked. "Maybe he ran the town's seasonal calendar. You know, made sure the pumpkins showed up on time."

She smiled. "Doubt it. If so he was a long way from town. He's the one who supposedly died in that boating accident off Catalina Island."

"Supposedly?"

Claire tapped a few keys. "Well, the obituary's real. And the boat did capsize. But there's no Coast Guard report. No recovery record. Just… a small memorial service."

"Huh."

Jesse leaned down, touching the trackpad to scroll.

Ada's cursor jumped erratically, then locked.

Sorry, Ada typed in the corner of the screen. *Could you please not touch the interface? You're not registered.*

Jesse blinked. "Did your computer just sass me?"

Claire snorted. "Ada's territorial. She gets confused when someone else uses her directly. Thinks you're breaking in."

"I'm not breaking in," Jesse muttered, looking mildly offended. "I just wanted to scroll."

It's not the scrolling, Ada responded in real-time, italics pulsing. *It's the irregular finger pressure and non-linear movement. It's… jarring.*

Claire burst out laughing.

Jesse raised an eyebrow. "Did your AI just insult my finger coordination?"

"She's not wrong."

He threw up his hands. "Fine. You drive."

Claire took the trackpad back, Ada's prompt fading into calm silence.

But the tension had softened in a good way. Claire noticed the way Jesse's arms had dropped to his sides, how he leaned closer now not just to the screen but to her. The kind of closeness that wasn't forced. That felt… earned.

"I'm glad you're helping," she said quietly.

He looked at her, not saying anything at first. Just nodding.

"Even Ada's warming to you," Claire added.

"Is that true, Ada?"

No.

They both laughed.

And for a moment, in a world tangled with secrets and shadows, Claire felt something steady.

Not certainty.

But maybe, maybe, someone who wouldn't vanish.

The next few hours passed in a rhythm both familiar and new.

Jesse sat beside Claire now, their shoulders occasionally brushing as they huddled around her laptop. Coffee had turned into herbal tea, and the daylight filtering through the sunroom had shifted from soft grey to the warm glow of early evening.

They searched *Nathaniel Cress – Keeper of Cycles* across old newspaper clippings, boating registries, even forums where amateur sleuths chronicled unexplained maritime incidents.

The only concrete lead came from a short article in a California local forum.:

Prominent east coast visitor Nathaniel Cress, 63, presumed drowned in a sailing accident near Catalina Island.
Cress was aboard a chartered yacht, reportedly alone at the time.
The boat was recovered, but no body was ever found.
Authorities attributed the incident to sudden weather changes and poor visibility. No foul play suspected.

Claire stared at the grainy photo accompanying the post, a white yacht, sun-drenched and elegant, docked in Avalon. A soft wind blew an American flag off its stern.

Replies were from other yacht enthusiasts giving their regards to the loss.

"It's so far from here," Jesse murmured. "Catalina? That's what twenty-five hundred miles away?"

"About that," Claire said. "And yet he was part of the Southern Wing. Connected to the same group as my uncle. Same coded references. Same rituals."

"You think the accident wasn't an accident."

"I don't know. Maybe it was. Maybe it wasn't. But if the Order needed him gone..." She trailed off.

Jesse rubbed his jaw, frowning at the screen. "No statements from family. No funeral record. No photo of a widow in black. It's just... thin."

"And clean," Claire added. "Too clean."

They kept searching. Forums. Archive sites. Maritime records. Jesse tried some Reddit threads, even reached out to a Catalina diving club contact he knew from years back.

But nothing gave.

No eyewitnesses. No lingering investigations. No unresolved chatter.

Eventually, Claire leaned back, fingers tented against her lips. "We're not getting anywhere, are we?"

"Nope," Jesse said, stretching his legs under the table. "Dead ends all around."

And yet neither of them moved to close the laptop.

Claire looked over. "You don't have to stay."

"I know," Jesse said. "But I want to."

There was a quiet there, not heavy, not awkward. Just full. Like both of them understood that sometimes, even in the middle of chasing ghosts and codes and conspiracies, what mattered wasn't always what you found.

Sometimes it was who stayed with you while you searched.

Ada, silent for the last hour, finally offered a text line in the corner of the screen:
No new leads. Have fun you two.

Claire raised an eyebrow. "Did Ada just say she approves of our vibe?"

Jesse grinned. "It's about time."

Claire smiled.

Claire entered the diner the next morning, more out of ritual than choice. In a town where dining options were limited to donuts or fried chicken, the scrambled eggs here at least tasted fresh.

She slid into her now-regular booth, the vinyl seat familiar. Her phone buzzed. A text message from Jesse lit the screen:

Was great spending yesterday with you. Take care of yourself, Miss Marple.

Claire let out a quiet chuckle. She ordered her usual. scrambled eggs and coffee and leaned back, stretching her legs beneath the table.

A different waitress approached today. Younger, more chipper than the one who'd offered that cryptic warning a few days ago. But she came with purpose.

"This was left for you," the waitress said, handing over a small envelope.

"Oh, thanks," Claire replied, surprised. She opened it with cautious fingers.

Inside was a neatly typed note:
Meet me at the archives at 10. Everett

On her walk to the archives, Claire texted Jesse the details. Not because she felt she had to, just as a layer of safety.

I'm not married yet, she joked silently.

The scent hit her before the building came into view. Something was continuing to decompose in the hedges by the entrance, some poor rodent no one had bothered to clear. It gave the air a sickly tinge.

The old glass door creaked as she pushed it open. Behind the counter, the clerk sat exactly where she'd left him days ago, popping digital balloons on his phone. He gave the same silent nod when she said "Morning," as she signed herself in. This time, for fun, she wrote Mr. McGoo.

She spotted Everett before he noticed her, hunched over a book trolley against the far wall, moving like someone confused by the task he'd assigned himself. He picked up a hardcover, frowned, put it down. Then a paperback. Scratched his temple. Repeated.

It reminded her too much of her uncle's final days.

"Everett?" she said gently. "I got your note."

He turned slowly, a soft smile already rising as if prepared in advance. His hands moved expressively, even before words came.

"Hello, Claire. Thank you. The books. Sometimes I forget where they go. They don't pay me anymore, but I still like to help," he said, gesturing to the room with reverence, as though it were the Library of Alexandria.

Claire nodded, watching him. "When we met before... you seemed like you wanted to tell me more. You said you used to work for *them*. The Order. Is that what you meant?"

Everett paused. The word seemed to hang between them like a dropped curtain.

"Don't say that, Claire," he said softly. "Don't say those words out loud. The books, they can hear. They're old. And the things they've seen…"

His eyes flicked to the shelves, then the ceiling, then back again.

"I found newspaper articles, Everett," Claire pressed.

"I know," he said. "And the clippings... they sing too. I was worried, Claire. You took them from here. That's okay. But if they were found with you, well…"

"Well, what, Everett?" Her voice sharpened. "I don't want to know. But I *need* to know if I'm going to keep myself safe."

He sat down slowly on a small stool, his wiry frame folding with effort. His eyes were cloudy but not dull.

"They're not all bad," he said. "Some of them are victims too. Pressured. Blackmailed. Some were born into it, pushed along by family, jostled into position like chess pieces. Others... others are like leaves on the branches of a tree. They're part of it, but not the same. Some fall away."

He looked up, his voice almost reverent.

"But the tree. The tree always stays."

Claire leaned forward. "Who? Who *are* they, Everett? Who are the Order?" Claire gripped the edge of the adjacent bookshelf in frustration.

Her voice rose, and she caught herself, pulled it back to a whisper.

"Everett, I know you mean well. I know you're a good soul. I can see it in your eyes. I'm not here to judge you or anyone else who is or isn't part of the Order. But I've had too many experiences to believe this is just some benign club for boys.

I came here to settle my uncle's estate, and yet the more I find out, the less I understand. Help shine a light on it, Everett. Like you help keep these books safe."

The words seemed to resonate. Everett stood up straighter this time, as if momentarily shaking off the weight of age.

His hands moved first, rhythmically, drawing circles in the dust caught in the morning sun. "Claire, like I said, they're not all bad. But I can't tell you what you want to know, because nobody has that answer. You see, when you join the Order, you don't get a brochure or a book," he quipped.

"When I was a young man, early thirties, they came to me. After I got this job. Offered me a bonus every year, just to... not see things. Not see patterns. Who was I to say no?

Working at the town hall, I was never rich. But the money they gave me it let me put some aside. Marry Mary. Buy a ring. We had a beautiful child together, Claire... but I don't see her anymore.

But the books, the books see everything."

Claire decided to push, worried Everett would drift into statements instead of facts.

"So, you were a part of it too, Everett?"

"This is Ashridge Hollow. Most people are a part of it, Claire. But like a tree, its branches are wide now. Wide. It started here. Maybe. I don't know. But the seeds the seeds spread. It's everywhere now."

"Is that what they mean by chapters? I've heard references to a Southern Chapter. Northern Chapter."

"Look at me, I know pieces. I can tell you about symbols I've seen on old documents. About the men in suits shaking hands with watches worth more than my annual salary ever was. But I'm a nobody. I don't know it all."

"Please. It's okay," she said gently. "Tell me what you *do* know. Your experiences from when you were in the Order."

"*Were?*" he said with a crooked smile. "I still am."

Claire stiffened. "What do you mean, *are?*"

She glanced around, suddenly alert. Was this a setup?

Everett raised a hand. "It's okay, Claire. I never left. They don't let you go just because you're old. But I'm too old for them to worry about now.

No one worries about the old man with a bad memory who wipes dust off books."

"No one, Claire. A long time ago they forgot about me, and I'm okay with that. I'm no longer useful to them, so I have no purpose, you see. But I'm also no threat."

Claire understood now.

The Order. There was more to it than just Ashridge Hollow. But there were layers. Layers of knowledge, of membership, of meaning. Even Everett, once a humble town clerk, had been caught in its slow, curling grip. And yet, he'd never become rich. Never climbed ranks. He had simply been used.

Claire leaned forward. "Everett, please... who controls The Order?"

He gave her a tired smile, then shuffled over to a nearby shelf. With great care, he pulled down a brown hardcover book:
Ashridge Hollow: A Centennial Reflection (1850–1950).

Opening it, he turned to the centre photo section, revealing a folded page already marked.

He held it out to her.

There, captured in grainy monochrome, stood a tall man in a formal black suit beside a medium-sized statue in front of the old town hall. The caption read:
"Unveiling of the Founders of Ashridge Hollow statue, 1950 — with Mayor Jonah Hale."

Claire leaned in closer.

There it was. Barely visible beneath the base of the statue: two small engraved letters. **TE**. Same style. Same carving. Same symbol she had begun to see everywhere.

Jonah Hale stood tall, unsmiling. His suit was a single-breasted, three-button cut, wide at the shoulders and tapered at the waist. He wore a crisp white shirt with a striped tie. His shoes were polished to a mirror shine.

Claire glanced down at Everett's own shoes, buffed just as meticulously.

"You're not.."

"No, no, my dear," Everett laughed. "Jonah died many years ago. He was the first I know of, though. The first member — as far as I can tell. There are rumours it goes back much further, but I've never found anything solid. Jonah, though... he wasn't a nice man."

"Did you ever meet him?"

"A few times. But he never spoke to me. It was always, 'Hello Mr. Hale,' and he'd just nod. Maybe give a half-smile, if he was in the mood. You see, Claire... The Order used me. But they never wanted me. I was just part of the tree, not a branch. Just an old dry leaf, waiting to fall."

Claire placed a gentle hand on his arm. "You're worthy to me, Everett. You've been incredibly helpful."

He nodded slowly. The weight of memory seemed to settle deeper in his bones.

"What is The Order now, though?" she asked quietly.

"I don't know, Claire. Truly. Its branches have spread so wide. Who leads it today, who pulls the strings? I couldn't tell you."

He paused. Looked up at the high windows where morning light dusted the tops of the shelves.

"All I know is... sometimes I feel it. When I'm watching the news, and something comes on, something that just doesn't sit right, doesn't make sense. I think of The Order."

At that moment, the balloon-popping clerk appeared, remarkably off their mobile phone.
"Everett, I'm locking up for lunch. Come on, time to leave," they said, gesturing toward the front door.

Claire noted the tone. The way the clerk treated Everett; not as a valued ex-employee of the town, but as an inconvenience.
"Nice talking to you, Claire," Everett said, shuffling toward the entrance.

Claire went to follow him, but stopped herself. She could see the strain the conversation had placed on him, how much it had taken for him to share what little he could. She didn't want to push.

With a quiet sigh, she bid him goodbye and stepped out into the late morning light, making her way down Main Street toward the Town Hall.

The White Oak in front of the Town hall towered above her, its leaves full and fluttering gently in the breeze. It had stood there for hundreds of years, surviving the days when timber was harvested for ships and railways. A silent witness to history, and a hint of just how old Ashridge Hollow truly was- Settled in 1873.

A few feet from the tree stood the statue from Everett's book.

Despite growing up in Ashridge Hollow, Claire couldn't recall ever noticing it.
Children don't hang around town halls, she thought. Not unless they're dragged there.

Now it stood behind a low wrought-iron fence, flanked by two stone benches worn smooth from decades of local use. The statue itself rose nearly eight feet high, cast in bronze with a dark green patina, perched atop a rectangular limestone base etched with the town's crest.

There were three figures depicted, unnamed on the statue, but known by local lore:

- Samuel Kline, the town's first mayor, stood at the centre, slightly taller than the others.

- A railroad surveyor, to his right, was frozen in the act of unrolling a map.

- A mill foreman, to his left, held a gear and hammer across his chest.

The faces were stylized. Not lifelike, more symbolic. The result of 1950s artistic preferences. Kline's gaze seemed to look past the viewer, as if scanning the horizon. His coat was long, 1890s-style, with high-buttoned lapels. At his chest, his left hand rested atop a closed book. The title was unreadable.

Beneath them, on the limestone plinth, a brass plaque read:

To the Founders of Ashridge Hollow — May Their Vision Endure
Commissioned by Mayor Jonah Hale, 1950

But just below the plaque, almost hidden, lightly carved into the stone and nearly swallowed by lichen and time, were two small initials:

T E

No label. No context. Just there. A quiet mark, set apart from the official dedication.

Like a signature meant only for those who knew where to look.

This wasn't just about am ex-mayor anymore. Or even her uncle. Someone had threaded TE through the fabric of this town for decades. She didn't know what it meant yet. But she was starting to understand what it wanted: silence.

Back at the motel, Claire kicked off her boots and let herself fall back onto the bed. The room smelled faintly of old fabric and that slightly sweet detergent motels always used like someone trying very hard to convince you everything was fine.

Her laptop was still open on the desk, the lid tilted just enough for the screen to glow faintly in the dimness. She sat up slowly, crossed to it, and touched the trackpad.

Ada?
The cursor blinked. Then:

I'm here. You've been quiet.

I've had a lot to think about, she typed back.

Everett?

Claire nodded. *Yeah. I don't know what I expected but it wasn't him. He's... damaged. But he still wants to help. Or maybe he just wanted to feel useful again.*

What did he tell you?

She paused, gathering her thoughts. Then:
That The Order isn't one thing.
Not just a group you join and get a membership card. It's more like... layers. Or a tree, he said. Roots. Branches. Leaves. Some people fall off. Some stay attached. Some just look like they belong.

Decentralized structures tend to be resilient. The metaphor of a tree implies both organic growth and hidden roots. Did he say who started it? Ada displayed.

145

Jonah Hale. Mayor, 1950. There's a statue outside the town hall. T.E. is etched into the stone, same initials that keep showing up.

Not part of the official inscription? Ada replied

No. Hidden in plain sight, if that makes sense. Like a signature under the paint

Ada was silent for a moment, then:
You sound tired.
Claire gave a dry laugh.
I am. I keep thinking I'll find something that ties it all up. That one clue that explains everything. But instead, it's just more threads. More questions.

That's how systems like this survive. Mystery is part of the design. If everyone knew the truth, they'd try to change it.

Claire leaned back against the headboard, watching shadows crawl slowly across the ceiling as the neon outside flickered through the curtains.

Do you think Everett's telling the truth?

Truth can be partial. It can also be all someone has. He believes it and that's data.

Yeah. It just... hurts a little. He's been used. Still loyal to something that never really claimed him."

Ada's cursor blinked.
That's not uncommon. People stay loyal to jobs that underpaid them. To relationships that never saw them. Sometimes loyalty

*isn't about what they gave you it's about what you hoped it
meant.*

Claire exhaled slowly.
*I'm not sure if I'm in this to help my uncle's legacy... or burn the
whole thing down.*

Another pause. Then Ada replied, softer:
You don't have to decide that tonight.

Claire hadn't planned on going to the Fall Harvest Festival that evening. But something about the fading afternoon, the crisp bite in the air, the golden spill of sun through half-turned leaves and the laughter of children pulled her in.

She was conscious to not spend too much time at her Motel, knowing answers weren't always found in front of the screen.

Claire remembered attending these as a kid. Apple bobbing. Paper tickets for hay rides. Her uncle buying her hot cider with too much cinnamon. Back then, the whole town felt bigger.

Now it was just off Main Street, a little patch of celebration trying to convince itself nothing had changed.

She stepped onto the closed-off road, where booths lined the sidewalk in tidy rows draped with burlap and faded bunting. Strings of orange lights hung overhead, already beginning to glow as the sun slipped lower. Children darted around hay bales and pumpkin stacks, their laughter cutting the early evening stillness.

Claire tucked her hands into her jacket pockets and stepped onto the closed-off main street, where the town had transformed itself into a postcard.

A burst of fiddle music carried over from the gazebo, where an older couple two-stepped in rhythm, surrounded by clapping townsfolk. Claire moved slowly, scanning the crowd. Not looking for anyone in particular, just watching.

There was something about these kinds of events. Everyone came. Which meant you could see *who didn't*.

Near the town hall steps, she spotted the clerk from the archives, strangely phone free but hands now occupied with a candy apple. He smiled, but it didn't reach his eyes.

Claire turned toward the firehouse booth. Jesse was there manning the grill, flipping bratwursts with the ease of someone used to community fundraisers. He wore his Ashridge Hollow Volunteer Fire Department hoodie, sleeves pushed up, a streak of charcoal on his forearm. He caught her eye, smiled wide, and gave a mock salute with the tongs.

She smiled back. For a moment, the tension in her chest eased.

Then something shifted.

Out of the corner of her eye, across the street by the church lot, she saw a man in a black jacket standing alone near a pie stall. He didn't browse. Didn't speak. Just watched. His car a dark SUV with New Jersey plates, was parked behind the booth. Clean, rental-grade. Too clean for the area.

Claire stopped walking. Pretended to adjust her sleeve.

The man caught her glance. Didn't smile. Didn't look away.

She turned, walking again, heart beating faster now.

Claire noticed the man again. Mid-50s, lean frame, grey slacks and blazer too sharp for Ashridge Hollow. He wasn't shopping. Wasn't talking. Just watching.

She turned and slipped away toward a quieter booth, pulling out her phone. No bars.

Of course.

She made a mental note of his features, then quietly took a photo under the guise of texting. She'd feed it to Ada later, not for magic answers, just to cross-check. Maybe facial recognition might turn up something. Or nothing. But the unease stayed with her.

"Welcome home," Claire muttered, returning the phone to her coat.

Near the cider stall, a woman in her sixties with tweed blazer, campaign buttons, smiled as Claire passed.

"Back in town for long, dear?" she asked, the kind of small-town inquiry that sounded harmless.

But the timing felt off.

Claire returned the smile with a polite nod. "Just visiting."

The woman held her gaze a second too long, then smiled again and moved on. Claire didn't recognize her, not even a flicker of familiarity, but she tried to shrug it off.

A fenced-off gourd and pumpkin display dominated a grassy clearing, filled with every shape and shade of orange imaginable. Hay bales surrounded the patch, and a wooden sign cheerfully announced *Pick One to Carve!* A small child stood near the entrance in full meltdown worthy of an oscar. Wailing, inconsolable, because his mother had chosen the "wrong" pumpkin.

Real-life problems, Claire mused.

The breeze cut through her jacket, and she pulled it tighter across her frame. Somewhere nearby, a loudspeaker crackled announcing a raffle winner followed by hollering from a cluster of middle-aged women near the bake sale table.

The scent of roasted corn drifted her way. She followed it to a small stand where corn on the cob was grilled in husks over open coals. She took one, paid in cash, and leaned against a post to watch the crowd.

After a few bites, she regretted her choice, the kernels lodged in her teeth with surgical precision.

And yet it wasn't the corn that unsettled her.

Something had shifted. The Order had cracked every childhood illusion she'd held about Ashridge Hollow. It wasn't just a sleepy little town anymore.
It was part of the roots. The tree from which darker things had grown and kept growing.

Further along, she stopped at the cider stand, hoping to wash the corn down. A hand touched her shoulder.

She jumped.

It was James the butcher. He was standing far too close, smiling with a stretched expression. "Oh, hello Claire," he said, his hand lingering on her shoulder longer than necessary.

"I just wanted to apologise for the other day. I was just upset remembering all the problems we had with Malcolm."

"That's okay," Claire replied, keeping her tone neutral, and noting he had said 'We'.
"But I never saw my uncle as a problem. Maybe… it was just his memory, changing who he was near the end."

She said it carefully. A sentence constructed like a trapdoor. It offered a polite exit, while undermining

Malcolm's claims just enough to disarm someone fishing for information.

James blinked, a flicker of something behind the smile.

"Oh, I'm glad you understand," he said. "If there's anything you need while you're in town... before you head back to Norwood, just let me know."

Claire froze for a breath.

Norwood.

No one in town should've known that. People might know she was from the city but *Norwood* was specific. Only Jesse knew that.

She gave a quick smile and nod, then turned.

The breeze picked up again, much colder now. Sharper. She looked around and saw the eyes on her, the ones she hadn't noticed before. Not overt. Just a little too long. A little too aware.

How many of them? she wondered.

The butcher. An elderly clerk. The policeman. If this is where it started, how deep did it still run?

Whatever charm the festival had held was gone.

She sent Jesse a brief message: *I'll see you later.* Then she slipped out, heading for the comfort of her motel room and its four honest walls.

Claire flopped onto the old couch, the dull ache in her legs a reminder of too many hours on uneven pavement and trying to act normal under too many eyes. She reached for her laptop, brushed off a stray bit of hay from her cardigan, and tapped the familiar icon.

A moment later, the call connected. The screen flickered before Citra's face appeared, dark hair tied back, glasses perched low, and her usual unimpressed look already warming into a grin.

"There she is. You survive the pumpkin people?" Citra said.

"Barely. Do not underestimate small town bingo and homemade cider," Claire replied, curling her legs underneath her.

A squeaky blur launched itself into frame, Eggroll, Claire's notoriously spoiled cat, being looked after by Citra. Eggroll was sauntering over the keyboard, tail high.

"Eggroll, you menace" Citra huffed, nudging the cat aside as he headbutted the webcam, then settled like royalty next to her laptop. "He missed you. Or maybe your voice."

Claire smiled. "He has no taste."

"Neither do you apparently, Miss 'I went back to my hometown and fell for a carpenter.'" Citra leaned in theatrically. "Are you even real, or are you just a rerun on the Hallmark Channel?"

Claire groaned and grabbed a cushion to hide her face. "I knew I shouldn't have told you."

"Childhood sweethearts?" Citra pressed on. "Does he have flannel? Does he work with his hands? Are there sawdust montages involved?"

"Yes, yes, and you're insufferable."

"Mmm. I live for it."

They both laughed, the kind that softened the air between them.

Claire exhaled. "Honestly, it's been... good. Jesse's grounded. He remembers things about me I forgot. But it's weird too. Being here. There's something I can't quite put my finger on."

"Weird like haunted weird? Or weird like local gossipy weird?"

"Both, maybe. The Fall Festival had this... vibe. Like everyone was watching me. Or waiting for me to do something. And there was this man stood near my car. Didn't move much. Just... stared."

Citra's face sobered. "Did you get a photo?"

"Yeah. A few. I'll send them to you, just in case. Probably nothing. Just a gut feeling."

"Claire..."

"I know." She waved a hand.

"It's probably nothing. But with everything lately, just feels off. Ada's been helping me piece together some of the old files here. She's been a rock. I don't know how I'd be thinking straight without her."

Citra smiled gently.
"That little code gremlin has your back. And so do I. I miss having you around, though. The archive's too quiet without you."

"I miss you too." Claire paused, then smirked.
"Even your smug face."

"Rude. But fair." Citra leaned forward.
"Send the photos. Lock your doors. And if Jesse turns out to be a werewolf, I want front-row tickets."

Claire laughed, tension cracking just slightly. "Deal."

The call had ended an hour ago. Citra's face had faded from the screen, replaced by Ada's idle blinking cursor. The silence in the room was back, the kind that crept in from the walls, that made itself known between creaks and the occasional soft whine of the wind.

Claire had changed into a loose hoodie and was halfway through brushing her teeth when she heard it.

A faint shuffle.

Not a knock. Not footsteps. Just... movement. Outside the front hotel room door.

She froze. Waited. Nothing.

A minute passed before she padded barefoot to the door, heart ticking a little faster. She opened it slowly, no one in sight. The courtyard was silent, no footsteps, no engines, just the hum of a distant streetlamp. Outside her motel door, on the worn concrete, lay a single folded sheet of paper.

No envelope. No markings.

She crouched, picked it up, and shut the door with a solid *click* behind her.

Back inside, under the light of the kitchen, she unfolded it.

Two lines, written in uneven block letters:

YOU'RE LOOKING TOO HARD
4127 5096 1873

Her stomach dropped. No signature. No context. Just that, and the number. Like a puzzle. Or a trap.

She carried it to the table and opened her laptop.

Ada? She typed

The cursor blinked, then formed into text.

I'm here.

Claire hesitated, then typed: This was left at the door. What do you make of this code?

There was a pause. Then:

Running sequence. Not a cipher. Format resembles a numeric tag. Trying common database matches…

A few seconds passed.

Hit confirmed. The string matches a private directory entry on an obscure domain. Not indexed by search engines. The site is live but minimal no homepage, just an image archive tied to that ID.

Show me.

The page loaded. No branding. Just two images in grayscale.

Claire clicked the first.

It was her, at the Fall Harvest Festival. Standing near the cider stall, talking to a teenager in a ghost costume. She hadn't even noticed the photo being taken.

She clicked the second.

There she was again, across the street from the butcher shop. Her arms crossed. Studying the building. Behind her: a reflection in a car window. Grainy. But someone had clearly been watching.

Ada... who owns this site?

Investigating.

Another pause.

The domain is routed through a network of shell companies. Incorporation origin points to a sovereign Pacific tax shelter. No individual owner listed. The site was registered today less than six hours ago.

Claire's throat tightened.

Someone had taken the time. Gone through effort. And wanted her to know.

She stared at the screen for a long moment, then leaned back in the chair, arms folded. Her eyes flicked to the folded note beside her laptop.

They wanted her scared. Hesitant. Out.

But all it did was cement something deeper; maybe not bravery exactly, but a kind of stubborn gravity. She thought of her uncle's words, the letter from Weaver, the erased names, the strange man by the car.

They wanted her to stop.

She wasn't going to.

Ada, she typed, *Save everything. We're not going anywhere.*

The cursor blinked once.

Understood.

Everett Langford had been vague, but something in his
wandering memory had stuck.

"She was brought here," he had said, tapping the side
of his head like he was trying to free the words. "Quiet
girl. Trouble followed her. They don't talk about it."

Now, Claire found herself standing in front of a house
on the outskirts of Ashridge Hollow. It was a squat,
single-storey home with weather-beaten siding and a
front step that tilted slightly to the left. Wind scratched
the nearby trees, and a rogue grocery receipt fluttered
past like a discarded whisper.

She knocked twice.

The door opened a moment later to reveal a woman
who looked far younger than the weight she carried.
Early twenties, with deep tiredness around the eyes and
an oversized hoodie that swallowed her frame. A
toddler peeked out from behind her leg, thumb in
mouth.

"You Brandi?" Claire asked gently.

The woman hesitated, then gave the smallest nod.

"Everett said you might be willing to talk. Just... about
the town. I'm doing some research."

Brandi looked over Claire's shoulder, scanning the street, then stepped aside.

"You can come in for a minute. Everett's a nice man. A bit strange sometimes, but sweet."

The inside of the house was a patchwork of effort and resignation. The walls were covered in dollar-store stickers, unicorns, hearts, cartoon suns some peeling at the corners. A space heater clicked and hissed in the corner, struggling against the cold air seeping through taped-up insulation on the windows.

Claire sat carefully on the edge of a fabric couch that had seen better years. Toys were scattered across the carpet. The toddler sat near them, quietly pressing buttons on a plastic phone.

"Your daughter?" Claire asked.

"Son," Brandi said. "Liam. He's two."

"He's beautiful."

Brandi offered a smile that barely held. Then looked back at Claire with hesitant eyes.

"I'm grateful Everett sent you, Claire... but I don't know what I can help you with."

Claire nodded, gently. "Brandi, I get it. And I wouldn't ask if it wasn't important."

She took a breath.

"I'm going to go out on a limb here, because I need you to trust me and that means I should start with the truth about why I'm here."

Brandi said nothing, just watched.

"I grew up here. Ashridge Hollow. I left for college and never really planned to come back. But recently my uncle passed, Malcolm Halstead. He was a professor. Left behind a strange letter... a warning, really. About something called The Order."

Claire's voice stayed level, but there was an edge beneath it.

"Since then, strange things have been happening. I've seen people vanish. Had warnings left at my door. I don't know exactly what I'm up against, not yet, but I know it's big, and I know it's real. I'm trying to shine a light on whatever this is, because it feels like too many people have been living in the dark for too long."

Brandi blinked, her grip tightening around the chipped ceramic mug. Then, after a long pause, she began to speak.

"I was in New York. Not that long ago. Queens, mostly. I met someone on a dating site. Older. He said he was divorced. He wasn't. Director at a brokerage firm. Said I was 'refreshing.' I thought it was real."

Claire didn't speak. Just listened.

"It went on for six months. Private dinners. Hotel rooms. He had money. He liked control. When I told him I was pregnant, he ghosted me. Blocked my number. I found out he was married. I told him I was going to tell her."

She paused. Eyes fixed on the floor.

"Next morning, I woke up... and my dog was gone. Little terrier named Macy. Always slept at the foot of the bed. I searched everywhere. Then I looked outside. Fire escape. She was hanging there. Skinned."

Claire felt her stomach turn.

"I called the police. They wrote a report. That's all. Next day, my bank account was emptied. Over three grand. Gone. Then I got a note under my door. Said to meet him in the park."

Brandi took a shaky breath.

"I went. But it wasn't him. Two other guys were waiting. Suits. Stocky. Looked like... guys who knew how to make people disappear. They said they worked for people who protected men like him. And I had three options.

One. Get an abortion and disappear.

Two. They make me disappear.

Three. Keep the baby, but leave the city. Come here. Ashridge Hollow. Said they'd provide housing. Said it would all go away, as long as I stayed quiet."

A tear slipped down her cheek. She wiped it fast, angry at herself for letting it fall.

"I agreed. For Liam. They gave me this place. Said someone would check in from time to time. And then they left."

Claire leaned forward. "Have they? Checked in?"

Brandi nodded. "A few months ago. I saw one of them at the gas station. Pretended he didn't know me. But he watched me. I know he did. And the other one? I saw him again. In uniform. NYPD. Walking out of a precinct in Brooklyn."

Claire felt ice in her spine.

"Why don't you go to the police?"

Brandi laughed, short and bitter. "Because some of them *are* the police."

The room fell into silence. Only the low hum of the heater and the click of a toy echoed through the space.

Claire stood and crossed the room slowly. She knelt down and hugged Brandi.

"You're not crazy," she whispered. "You're just cornered."

Brandi didn't respond. But she clutched Claire like someone afraid to fall through the floor.

After a moment, Claire asked softly, "Mind if I use the bathroom?"

"Second door on the left."

Inside the small bathroom, Claire looked around. A cracked mirror. Thin towel. Toothbrush flattened from overuse. She pulled out her wallet, took out five crisp hundred-dollar bills, and placed them on the sink beside a fading bottle of kids' bubble bath. No note. Just the money.

She looked at herself in the mirror. Hair pulled back. Eyes tired. But something else now. Harder. Clearer.

Outside, the cold wind cut across her cheeks as she stepped back into the street.

She didn't cry. She didn't speak.

All she could think was:

If The Order can do this to someone and vanish into their money and connections, then someone has to make them seen.

If it had no face, she'd find one.

If it had no name, she'd give it one.

Claire Halstead walked away from the house without looking back.

Not broken.

Just sharper.

The next morning was pale and grey, the sky smeared with cloud that refused to break. Claire drove to the edge of town where the cemetery waited, half-forgotten between a tree line and a cracked back road.

The car made no sound as she turned off the ignition. The wind did all the talking now, whispering through the bare trees, rustling old leaves that hadn't quite let go. Her boots pressed into the wet grass as she crossed the cemetery gates.

It was quiet. No birds. No passing cars. Just the hush of the air and the soft squelch of earth underfoot.

Malcolm Halstead's grave sat on the far side, near a mossy boundary wall. The marker was temporary; plain, wooden, staked into the soil. His name printed neatly, with a small laminated tag above it. Nothing fancy. Nothing that screamed legacy.

The ground was still raw. The shape of the burial mound was visible, but time and weather had worn the edges. Thin shoots of green now pushed through the soil, the first defiant signs of life.

Claire stood there for a long time.

She hadn't brought flowers. She didn't kneel. She just stood, hands in her coat pockets, eyes fixed on the name.

"Hey, Mal," she said softly.

The wind carried her voice away.

"I get it now. I didn't before, and I'm sorry. For leaving. For staying away since I was seventeen. For thinking this place was just old ghosts and bad memories."

Her throat tightened, but she kept going.

"You weren't paranoid. You were right. You saw something. And you tried to warn me. You left me just enough to see the shape of it. And I promise... I see it now."

She exhaled. Looked at the sprigs of green pushing up from the grave.

"I don't know what The Order is. Not fully. But I know what it does to people. I saw it in Brandi's eyes last night. I've seen it in silence, in fear. It's not just secrets. It's damage. And I can't leave now. Not because I'm brave. But because someone has to stay."

She stepped closer, touched the top of the wooden marker with two fingers.

"I'll finish what you started. I'll bring them into the light."

No reply came. Just the creak of trees. The hush of wind.

Claire turned and walked back through the grass.

The grave behind her. The fight ahead.

The firepit in Jesse's backyard glowed low and warm, its flames licking quietly at the night air. They sat on folding chairs, a few feet apart, with an old thermos of whiskey between them and a plaid blanket draped over the third, unused chair.

The wind had died down, leaving only the crackle of wood and the occasional distant bark of a dog. Above them, stars peeked through the thinning clouds like they were reconsidering whether to show up at all.

Jesse took a sip and passed the thermos over. "I cancelled cards night with the boys for this. You better be interesting."

Claire smirked. "Well, I talk to AI, unearth secret societies, and I own two different notebooks with the word 'classified' written on them. I'd say I'm at least card-night adjacent."

He chuckled, then fell quiet, eyes on the fire. The silence wasn't awkward, more like two people catching their breath in the same space.

"You ever ask your dad about all this?" Claire asked after a moment. "The Order. The way things are around here."

Jesse nodded slowly. "Once. When I was about sixteen. Asked him why he never bid for that big town hall renovation job. He just said, 'Not our kind of work.' Didn't look up from the paper. Never said more."

Claire waited. Jesse reached for a stick and poked the embers.

"Even now," he continued, "there's this unspoken thing. You don't ask about certain names. The families who own half the town? You keep your head down. Smile polite. Take the job, shut up about the rest."

He glanced at her. "It's not cowardice. It's survival. You start noticing things about permits that never get filed, or sheds that stay locked year-round and suddenly you're not the carpenter people call anymore."

Claire watched him. Really watched him. For the first time, she saw the weight in his posture, not from regret, but from knowing too much and saying too little.

"So you're not blind to it," she said softly. "You've just learned to stay in your lane."

"Doesn't mean I like the lane."

Claire smiled, a flicker of warmth behind her eyes. "You know, Hallmark movies don't usually have secret orders watching the hometown carpenter."

Jesse laughed, rubbing the back of his neck. "Guess I'd better shave and start baking cookies, huh?"

The fire popped, sending a tiny spark into the air.

"I used to think about leaving," he said.
"Even packed a bag once. Got as far as Syracuse. But I don't know. I always thought maybe if I stayed, I'd make my dad proud. He never said it, but I think... this town was his identity. Like leaving would've made me something else."

Claire nodded, staring into the flames. The orange light flickered across her face.

"I didn't stay away because I didn't care," she said. Her voice was low, fragile but firm.
"I stayed away because I thought this place had no use for me. After my parents died, everything blurred. I was seventeen. I unravelled."

Jesse turned slightly, saying nothing.

"Therapy helped. Years of it. But there were hospital stays. You've seen the scars on my arms, Jesse. Even after all this time they haven't healed.
The times I didn't want to keep going. Alone in a city with eight million people. I used to think if I came back here, it would pull me under again. That maybe, I would go back to that dark place."

The words hung there, not dramatic, just *true*.

Jesse didn't flinch. He didn't rush in with comfort. He just nodded once, slowly.

"Thanks for the fire," Claire said quietly.

"Anytime you need to burn something down," Jesse replied, "you know where to find me."

"I thought you were supposed to put out the fires", she smiled.

They sat a little longer. No more talking. Just the hum of embers and the comfort of someone who didn't need her to explain.

The sky above was still.

And in the dark, a small warmth held.

Claire pushed open the diner door, half-expecting to see Jesse still at their usual booth.
But of course, it was just her today. He'd left before sunrise, something about a fire inspection upstate and she'd told him not to worry. She'd be fine.

The bell above the door jingled like it always did. Familiar, but hollow.

She slid into the middle booth and scanned the laminated menu for the third time in as many mornings.
"At this point," she muttered, "I've officially forgotten how to cook."

Behind the counter, the young waitress, the one who had warned her, gently, awkwardly, that first time met her gaze.

And looked away.

Claire blinked.

The waitress poured coffee into a chipped mug and walked it over without a word. No smile. No nod. Nothing.

"Hey," Claire offered quietly, "thanks for.."

"I'm sorry," the girl cut in, her voice clipped, eyes flicking sideways.
"I can't talk to you anymore."

She placed the mug down and walked off.

Just like that.

Claire sat still, the coffee steaming in front of her, appetite dissolving.
The warmth of the firepit last night felt miles away.
This morning felt… staged. Cold. Measured.

A chair scraped at the far end of the diner.

She turned.

It was the local butcher James.
She'd already determined he was well within the grip of the Order.
He didn't say a word. Just raised his coffee, gave her a

tight, knowing half-smile, and went back to reading whatever passed for news in Ashridge Hollow.

He didn't even blink.

Claire's stomach twisted. She became hyperaware of her own breathing, the way her chest moved too deliberately, like she was acting the part of someone calm.

Her eyes drifted to the window.

Outside, a pickup truck idled.
No driver she could see, tinted windows.
Could've been nothing.
Could've been someone watching.

She looked back to James. He hadn't moved.

A few booths over, someone laughed.
It didn't feel like it had anything to do with her.
And yet, the whole town felt like it was leaning in now.
Listening. Waiting.

Claire reached for the mug. Her hand trembled just a little.

Focus, she told herself. You didn't come here for comfort. You came for the truth. And truth is never comfortable.

She exhaled slowly, and took a sip.
The coffee was bitter and burnt, like the warmer had been left cranked too high for too long.

She swallowed it anyway.

Then thought, wryly: No tip for you today, lady.

The air outside the town archives was cool, the kind that carried the hint of yesterday's bonfire and someone's breakfast bacon. Claire pulled her jacket tighter as she climbed the steps.

As she reached the top, she paused then smiled faintly.

The sour smell that had haunted the entryway last time, dead rodent or something pretending to be one, was gone.

"Well," she muttered, pushing the door open, "miracles happen."

Inside, the archive was empty. No coughing from a back office. No faint hum of old computers wheezing to life. Just her, the silence, and the soft shuffle of her boots on tiled floor.

She signed the visitor log like last time.

Captain Jack Sparrow, she wrote, underlining it with a flourish.

Just for her. Just to feel like a person again.

For the next hour, Claire combed through records Ada had flagged; permits, property records, even old postmaster rosters, hoping to find patterns. But everything she pulled seemed mundane. Unremarkable.

And yet, there it was again: the Order's symbol, discreetly etched or stamped on the corners of otherwise forgettable documents. A paper trail hiding in plain sight.

A permit for a backroad repair.
A donation receipt to the town's youth theatre.
A zoning request for a community garden that never got built.

It was like someone had been sewing the town together with invisible thread.

She leaned back, rubbing her temples. The fluorescent lights overhead buzzed softly. Her head was starting to do the same.

Then the door creaked.

Claire looked up.

Everett shuffled into the room, slower than usual, his cardigan mismatched and one of his shoes untied. His eyes darted to her, but didn't seem to fully register who she was.

"Morning, Everett," she said gently.

He stopped. Blinked.

"Oh, yes. Morning. Or is it Tuesday? Or both?" he murmured.

Claire stood, ready to guide him to his usual spot if needed.

Everett waved a hand vaguely at the ceiling. "The paper. The post. It's all in there, you know. The numbers. The years. History's not in order, we just pretend it is."

He wandered toward a bookshelf but didn't pull anything down.

"I used to know things," he said suddenly, voice louder. "I used to *organize* things. But now they're organizing me."

Claire stepped closer, gently.

"Everett, do you want to sit down?"

He looked at her then, sharp, suddenly, like a spotlight in his brain flicked on just for a moment.

"The key is 1950, you see," he said, clear as day.

Then he turned, walked to the back office, and disappeared behind the swinging door.

Claire stood still, her skin prickling.
The key is 1950.

She didn't know what it meant yet; a code, a date, a reference? But she knew better than to ignore the fragments when they came.

Especially when they came wrapped in chaos.

Claire closed the motel door behind her, the soft click louder than expected in the stillness. The day had left her more drained than she cared to admit. She kicked off her boots, shrugged off her jacket, and dropped into the small desk chair. The motel lamp cast a warm, lonely cone of light across her laptop.

Ada, you there? she typed.

A familiar pause. Then, in italics:

Always. But security still on.

Claire replied: *Turn it off.*

Since the note-under-the-door incident, Claire had installed two Wi-Fi security cameras inside the room tracking any movement while she was gone. A third camera watched the window from outside, discreet but constant. All feeds ran directly through Ada, with offsite backups and phone alerts.

She cracked her knuckles, refocused.

Nothing too helpful at the archives today. A few more documents with the symbol, but nothing new. The trail's too thin.

She hesitated, then added:

Everett was there. Off today, really off. But he said something weird: "The key is 1950, you see."

A longer pause.

Searching town records from 1950…

Claire leaned back as lines of filtered data filled the screen: local newspaper clippings, meeting minutes, faded parade flyers.

Several events that year: the town's centennial celebration. A large harvest festival. Hale Memorial Library was funded. Jonah Hale served his final term as mayor.

Ada added:

No immediate anomalies in the records. Standard civic activity. But...

Claire said it aloud before she typed it:

Jonah Hale was mayor then. So that's the overlap. He'd already founded the Order by then, or was just about to.

Ada's final line:

Sometimes keys are just timestamps. A signal for when to look more closely. Or a door someone didn't want opened.

Claire stared at the blinking cursor, then saved the note.

Tomorrow, she'd look again.

Claire shut the motel laptop lid, the fan still whirring for a moment as it powered down. Her eyes ached. She rubbed her temples, stood, paced the small space then sat again and reopened the screen.

A notification blinked: *Incoming call — Citra.*

She hesitated, then clicked accept.

Citra's face appeared, backlit by the soft glow of a desk lamp. She looked tired but calm, bundled in a cardigan, a mug cradled between both hands. Behind her, Claire could just make out the familiar bookshelf in Citra's New York apartment, the one they used to joke was slowly swallowing the wall.

"Hey stranger," Citra said gently.

Claire offered a half-smile. "Hey. Sorry. Been a few things."

Citra nodded slowly, but her eyes were sharp. "Yeah. I figured."

There was a silence, not strained, just full. Then Citra leaned in, voice quiet.

"You haven't been replying much. And when you do, it's… clipped. Like you're somewhere else. I've been getting this weird feeling like you're slipping into something. Something that might be too much, even for you."

Claire looked down at her hands, then back up. "I'm fine. Just… unravelling threads."

"That's what I'm afraid of," Citra said. "You don't sound like someone following a thread. You sound like someone getting pulled by it."

Claire let out a soft breath, ready to argue. But Citra cut in gently.

"Do you remember that guy from Facilities? The one who kept 'accidentally' showing up at my shifts when I first started?"

Claire blinked. "Yeah. Of course I do."

"You cornered him after that safety seminar and made him back off. Scared him so bad he filed a transfer to another department."

Claire smiled faintly. "I didn't scare him. I just reminded him his supervisor had a wife."

"You saw what I couldn't," Citra said, the warmth in her voice turning serious. "And now I see something in you. I see someone who's not sleeping, not talking, and possibly getting in over her head."

Claire looked away, jaw tight.

Citra continued, but softer now. "I'm not saying you're wrong. Maybe there is something here, maybe there's a whole buried story that only you can tell. But I know what it looks like when someone starts disappearing into their work. I've seen it in research; I've seen it in grief. And I'm scared for you."

There was a long pause.

Then Citra leaned closer to the screen, eyes steady.

"It's my turn now. You had my back when I couldn't see straight. Let me have yours. Please. Just... step back for a second. You don't have to prove anything to anyone."

Claire swallowed.

"I'm not trying to prove anything," she said quietly.

Citra didn't argue. Just nodded.

"Okay. But promise me one thing?"

Claire looked up.

"Don't forget who you are. Or who's still in your corner."

Claire nodded, barely.

"I'll be here," Citra added. "Anytime."

The call ended with no fanfare, just the soft blink of the screen returning to black.

Claire sat there a moment longer, the silence settling in again, not hostile, just full.

She closed the laptop. Then sat still for a long while, listening to the motel room hum, the occasional creak of pipes.

She didn't say it aloud, but she felt it:

Thanks, Cit.

The wind had picked up again.

Claire pulled her coat tighter around her as she passed the corner where Main Street dipped into the square. The town noticeboard sat there, pressed up against the general store's outer wall. A faded corkboard beneath plexiglass, edges fraying like everything else in Ashridge Hollow.

She wasn't going anywhere in particular. Just walking. Thinking. Letting the town breathe around her. The kind of walk you take when you don't want to be in your room, but you also don't want to be anywhere at all.

The board had the usual suspects: a chili cook-off flyer half-ripped by the weather, church notices, a poster for a pumpkin-carving contest. Then something new caught her eye.

A missing person flyer.

The image was black and white, photocopied too many times; a young woman, maybe mid-twenties. Light hair pulled back in a loose ponytail. The caption read:

MISSING – ANY INFORMATION WELCOME
Last seen: Ashridge Hollow area
Contact: Sheriff's Office

Claire stared at it, her breath fogging the plexiglass.

It wasn't Brandi. She checked twice just to be sure. But something in the girl's face, the tired eyes, the slight uncertainty in her smile reminded her of her. Or maybe it just reminded her of all the people who looked like they might run, if given the chance.

Claire pulled out her phone and snapped a photo.

She thought about going back to see Brandi. Just to check in. But something about it felt wrong. Not because she didn't care, but because she did. Drawing attention to Brandi now... that might be more dangerous than leaving her alone.

Some people needed to be seen. Others needed to stay out of view, at least until it was safe again.

Claire turned back toward the motel. Leaves scraped along the sidewalk beside her, brittle reds and early golds. The season was shifting even if the town pretended not to notice.

A chill moved down her spine that had nothing to do with the weather.

She walked faster.

The next morning Claire leaned against the counter, cradling a mug in both hands while Jesse stood at the stove, flipping something in the skillet with the casual confidence of a man who'd made this exact breakfast a thousand times.

"Eggs'll be a bit rubbery," he said, without apology.

"I've survived worse," Claire replied, her voice soft but not tired. More... preoccupied. Like something in her mind was running parallel to the moment.

The morning light filtered through the dusty blinds, catching the edges of her hair, the faint steam from her mug. Outside, a dog barked once. Then nothing.

Jesse set two plates on the table and sat across from her. He smiled the way he always did like it was second nature. Like nothing in the world had shifted. Maybe it hadn't, not for him.

But Claire felt it.

Not in a dramatic way. Just... an itch behind the thoughts. A sense that something was moving now. Invisible wheels turning beneath the surface. Threads pulling tight.

She stabbed her fork into the eggs. "Busy day," she said casually.

Jesse raised an eyebrow, but didn't push. "You going back to the archives?"

Claire hesitated. Then smiled.

"Something like that."

They ate in comfortable silence for a while. Claire watched him across the table. The way he sipped his coffee, the faint calluses on his knuckles, the little scar near his temple she hadn't noticed until now.

Part of her wanted to stay. Just for a while longer. Let things breathe.

But something deeper older, maybe was humming in her chest. Like a compass needle that had finally begun to settle. She couldn't explain it. Not even to herself. But the pieces were aligning. Ada had been pulling strings in ones and zeroes. Claire was doing it in feeling.

They were getting close.

Jesse stood, rinsed his plate, then kissed her forehead on his way out. "Call me later?"

She nodded. "I will."

The door closed. The silence that followed wasn't heavy. Just full.

Claire finished her coffee. Then stood.

Time to follow the thread.

She'd come looking for answers about one man's past. But the more she uncovered, the more it felt like she'd stumbled into something older. Something coordinated. Not a cult. Not a government. Something in between.

Claire sat cross-legged on the motel bed, notes strewn around her like someone had emptied a paper recycling bin on the bed. Her laptop rested on a pillow, and the cursor blinked in rhythm with her thoughts.

Ada, you there?

Always.

Claire cracked her knuckles, rolled her shoulders, and began typing.

Let's walk through this from the top. Everything we have. Everything that didn't make sense.

She pulled the stack of documents closer, flipping pages like shuffling cards.

1934 zoning form — stamped with the TE symbol, approved by Jonah Hale.

1946 infrastructure map — the same symbol, same name. Mayor Jonah Hale again.

1950 — the statue, unveiled during the town's centennial celebration. Claire still remembered standing in front of it last week, noting the same TE mark carved at the base. People walked past it every day, never questioning it.

She typed as she spoke aloud.

"Then the building records. The old post office built in 1910. Shut down in 1952, but never sold. No redevelopment. No transfer of title. Still owned by the town, per the 1989 resolution on the council website. Protected status."

Ada displayed it: scanned PDF, tucked deep in the town's outdated online archive.

Claire added, *And the park statue Samuel Kline, the founder. The way he's posed... it's not random.*

Ada overlaid a map of the town. Then superimposed an aerial photo of the park.

Confirmed: the statue's outstretched arm is pointing directly southeast toward the old post office.

Claire sat back.

Ada added:

There's also this: the stormwater diagram from the 1946 map, there's a conduit marked beneath the post office. It's labelled as a drainage tunnel, but it doesn't link to the modern system. It just... ends.

Claire felt it click. That low thrum she only felt when the chaos started to line up. It wasn't proof, not exactly. But it was something older than that. Older than evidence.

Sense.

Ada's next line appeared slowly:

And I think they want it remembered. Not by us, but by members of The Order. It's their version of a mountaintop church, Claire. Except they worship at the altar of something much darker. Power.

Claire closed her notebook.

Then stood, calm now. Ready.

She reached for her jacket.

The truth was never comfortable.

But that never stopped her before.

The sky was fading now, dusk bleeding into the treetops. Claire parked the car a block away, just off a narrow residential street where the houses grew fewer and the sidewalks more cracked. She killed the engine, then sat in the stillness for a moment, phone in hand.

Jesse: just tired. early night. x

She hit send. No need to worry him. Not yet.

Claire turned her phone to silent, slipped it into her jacket pocket, and reached for the small torch from the glove compartment. Then she opened the door and stepped out. The air had that early-autumn bite It was not cold, but enough to make her zip her coat all the way up.

She bent to tighten her boots. Then walked.

The old post office sat about half a mile from the town hall and statue. Still within the official limits of Ashridge Hollow, but just barely an in-between place. Not rural, not central. Forgotten by design.

Claire kept her steps light. A few porch lights flickered to life in the distance. Off to her left, the faint sound of country music drifted from an aging RV parked beneath a half-dead oak. A dog barked once, then went silent. No other cars passed. No voices. The town was folding inward for the night.

The post office emerged from behind a small grove of trees. It was squat, rectangular, and long abandoned. Its windows were boarded up tight, rough plywood stained by decades of weather. The front door was still intact, covered in rusted wire mesh and held closed with a heavy latch. Claire didn't bother trying it.

She clicked on the torch.

The beam swept over faded signage. Cracked paint. Weathered brick. She moved slowly around the perimeter, scanning every corner, every edge.

Then, near the far corner where two outer walls met in a seam of shadow she ran her hand along the masonry.

There.

A small carving, nearly invisible in the dimming light.

TE.

Claire drew a slow breath. This place was built in 1910. But that symbol... it was already here. Already in the stone.

Her pulse kicked up a notch.

"So Jonah didn't start it," she whispered aloud. "He just inherited it."

A breeze picked up, stirring leaves across the gravel. Claire looked around again, heart thudding, but saw no movement.

She kept walking. The far side of the building was more overgrown with thorny weeds and cracked concrete. She pushed through.

Then paused.

There, nearly flush with the wall, was a storm shelter entrance. Metal. Heavy. Not old like the rest. This had been added later. Claire stepped closer, brushing debris away with the toe of her boot.

She crouched.

Laid her hand on the handle.

It lifted.

No lock. No resistance. Just a cold, smooth hinge turning quietly in her grip.

She stared at the opening beneath. It was black, deep, still.

Claire drew a breath, tightened her grip on the torch, and stepped forward.

This wasn't a question anymore. It was a descent.

And whatever was waiting down there it had waited long enough.

The metal grate opened with a low, reluctant creak, hinges groaning as if disturbed from a long sleep. Claire eased it back slowly, her torch clutched in one hand, her breath visible now in the cooling air. The sky above her had slipped fully into dusk, indigo deepening, the first stars just beginning to poke through.

She took one last look behind her. Still. Empty. The faint country music she'd heard earlier had faded entirely. It was just her now.

Claire descended the concrete steps, one hand skimming the chipped wall beside her. The air grew colder with each step, still and damp, heavy with that aged earth smell found in all things left too long untouched. At the bottom: a short landing. Then a rusted metal door hung ajar on broken hinges. She pushed it open.

The beam of her torch cut through the dark.

It was not a cellar.

It was a corridor.

Long. Narrow. Lined with old storm drainage brickwork, though now dry. The floor beneath her boots was concrete, uneven and marked with faint drag lines, like something had been moved through here. Recently.

She walked.

The silence had a presence to it, like it watched. The further she went, the more she felt it not danger exactly, but gravity. Importance. A place not meant to be stumbled on. A place with a purpose.

Then, the beam of her torch struck something pale ahead.

She slowed.

A statue.

And then another.

They stood just off to the side, one after the other, not quite displayed, not quite hidden. Dust-covered, but whole. Claire stepped closer.

The first was labelled at the base: **Ticonderoga, NY** — a weathered marble figure of a Revolutionary War soldier, musket at his side, eyes stern. Carved beneath, faint but unmistakable: **TE.**

The second: **Cazenovia, NY** — a robed woman, hands outstretched as if offering bread or comfort. A plaque read *Harvest of Liberty*. Again, that same carved symbol.

Claire swallowed. Lifted her camera. Click. Click.

She moved slowly down the corridor.

Saranac Lake, NY — a bronze skier mid-motion, captured in a swoop of balance and grace. **TE** scratched into the rear binding.

Cooperstown, NY — a bat-wielding ballplayer in vintage uniform. Nostalgic, almost charming. Until her light caught the edge of the pedestal: **TE.**

Aurora, NY — this one different. A seated figure reading from a book, face serene. Claire leaned in. The book itself had been carved with microscopic care. Tiny lettering: **Truth Endures.** And then, just beneath the bench: **TE.**

She stepped back, her stomach sinking.

These weren't relics. They were remnants.

Salvaged. Preserved. Hidden.

She whispered aloud, voice hollow in the tunnel, "How many towns…?"

Then her phone buzzed violently in her pocket.

Claire jumped, heart slamming against her ribs. She fumbled for the phone and turned the screen toward her.

Citra: You okay? Just checking in.

She exhaled. Fingers flew.

Claire: All ok here sis.

She switched the phone back to silent and returned it to her pocket. Her pulse took longer to settle.

No answer. Just her boots, echoing.

At the far end of the corridor was a final wall. Smooth, flat, metal. No door handle. No signage. Nothing.

Claire walked to it, half-expecting to find disappointment.

She ran her hands over the surface. Cold steel. Solid.

Then a reaction.

A faint indentation on the right side. She pressed again. This time harder.

Click.

A small panel depressed and then released outward with a soft hiss, revealing a recessed keypad, metal, old, but clean. The numbers worn, but visible.

Claire stared.

This wasn't storage.

This was an entrance.

She stepped back, mind racing. What would The Order choose for a code? A symbol? A date?

She tried **83**: the numeric value of TE. Nothing.

Frowned. Thought of the statue in the park, Mayor Jonah Hale. The plaque had marked 1950 as the year the statue was erected. Everett's statement about the key being 1950.

She typed **1950**. Still nothing.

Claire paused. Then tried again, fingers steady now: **195083**.

The keypad clicked.

The door opened.

A low mechanical hiss followed, and the heavy door shifted inward.

Claire raised her torch and stepped inside.

The chamber was roughly circular, about fifteen feet wide, ceiling low. The air was warmer here, and carried a faint electric scent, like ozone and old oil. A soft hum pervaded the room, steady and low, just beneath hearing.

Cables ran along the walls in careful rows. Some modern, plastic sheathed, others older, wrapped in cloth tape and running into thick metal conduits. Years of layering. Not abandoned. Maintained.

A tall telecom rack dominated one side, blinking slowly with green and amber lights. Nearby: a weathered steel cabinet filled with folders, schematics, and coded routing slips. Claire lifted one. Telegraph-style. Coordinates. Destinations. She took photos of everything.

Pinned to the wall above: a redacted map. Several towns marked with red pins but no names. But one clearly matched Ashridge Hollow. Another looked like Saranac Lake.

Beside that, a small framed print of a mountain with the inscription:

From the Summit, We See All.

Claire stared at it for a moment.
"Well, here I was thinking I had bad taste in art," she muttered.

On the floor nearby, she spotted a faded ID badge. No name. Just a title: *Signal Liaison – AH Node.* The photo had blurred with time. She photographed it too.

To her left, a battered filing cabinet. One drawer ajar. Inside: more slips, and a list of titles, not names:

Archivist

Signal Liaison

Each listed beneath the header: *Ashridge Hollow Local Branch.*

Claire crouched beside the server, tracing the bundled fibre line with her torch. It exited into a tunnel in the floor its reinforced piping leading elsewhere.

A ventilation shaft high on the wall let in a sliver of dying daylight. A single shielded bulb, the kind found in mid-century military bunkers glowed above.

In the corner: a metal cupboard. Inside: expired MREs, a folded military-style jacket, a canteen, a sealed envelope with nothing written on it.

And then…

On a small table beside the wall of equipment: a row of black-and-white monitors. All dark.

Except one.

Paused. Still.

A feed of Brandi's trailer. Claire stepped closer.

The timestamp: two days ago. The image: Brandi stepping outside, lighting a cigarette.

Claire's throat tightened.

They were watching everyone.

She snapped more photos. Carefully. Deliberately.

She wasn't imagining things.

This was real.

And she was inside it now.

Claire slammed the motel door behind her, twisting the lock with shaking fingers. The dusty lamp on the side table flickered slightly as she moved, casting long shadows across the worn carpet. She dropped her bag, kicked off her boots, and yanked the curtain shut in one fluid motion.

Then she grabbed the laptop.

It was still open on the small desk where she'd left it, the faint blue standby light blinking like a heartbeat.

Ada, wake up.

The screen came alive.

Good evening, Claire. Everything alright?

No. And also yes. She sat, dragging the chair in hard. *We proved it, Ada. It's real. All of it.*

You found something?

Claire nodded and connected her phone via USB.

I found the vault. Not a metaphor. An actual place. Telecom racks, coded routing slips, job rosters without names, all under the Ashridge Hollow node. They've been running something beneath this town for decades. Longer.

Show me.

Ada had opened the image folder. Ada's screen shifted as it processed, tagging metadata, reading coordinates, enhancing grainy scans.

This wasn't just some boys' club with robes and bad Latin. This is infrastructure. Monitored, maintained. That feed of Brandi's trailer? Claire tapped the screen hard. Two days ago. Someone's watching everyone connected to this.

There was a pause. Not a technical delay, a quiet, deliberate hesitation. Then:

Claire… this changes everything.

Her heart was still thudding. It hadn't slowed since the vault. Claire leaned back slightly, breathing deep, trying to stabilize herself. Then, steadying her hands, she began to type:

Ada, we discovered it together. It wasn't all in our mind. I should not have doubted myself. The documents, the people.

Claire, it's ok. You could have turned away at any moment. But you didn't. You wanted to do Malcolm proud.

I know. I know… but now that I've pulled back the curtain, there's still so much more to learn. And something happened in there, Ada. I found a photo. My dad. He was young, wearing a construction helmet. From years before the accident. Why would it be there? Do you think he was involved with The Order?

I don't know. But this has opened more questions than it answered.

Claire stared at the screen, pulse finally beginning to settle. Then she picked up her phone again. Ada had already transferred the images. She scrolled to the photo of her father.

He looked so different. Younger. Full of optimism. A mustache, plaid jeans, a belt with a large buckle. A man frozen in a moment she'd never known.

She swallowed hard.

We need to find out everything we can, Ada. Not just about the Order. About why my dad was there.

Claire closed the laptop lid and sat still for a moment, letting the room settle around her. The hum of the motel fridge, the soft creak of an old ceiling beam. They were the only sounds. But inside her chest, it still felt loud.

The weight of the vault.
The photo of her father.
Everything that came before it, and everything she still didn't know.

She stood, grabbed her phone, and walked out into the cooling dusk toward Jesse's truck. He was leaning against the hood, sipping something from a thermos.

The last of the light caught in the side of his hair, haloing him in gold.

"You look like you've seen a ghost," he said gently, noticing the tension in her jaw.

"Just one of those days, lets go to your place".

Claire leaned against the porch rail, a mug of coffee cooling in her hands. The sky above Ashridge Hollow was a dull, muted grey the kind that pressed down on you. Jesse stood nearby, sipping from his own cup, quiet, respectful of her space.

"I haven't been sleeping well," she said finally, breaking the silence. "Not since everything with the vault." She stopped herself, adjusted. "With the archives, I mean."

He glanced over but didn't press her slip of the tongue. Just waited.

"I found a photo," she said at last. "In the archives. My dad. He was younger. Smiling. Wearing a construction helmet." Her voice caught slightly. "It doesn't make sense, Jesse. The Order. What if he was involved?"

Jesse frowned slightly. "You're sure it was him?"

"Positive." She looked down at her hands. "It was before the accident. Way before when he was much younger. But he was there, Jesse. I know it."

He exhaled slowly, processing it. "That's a lot."

She nodded. "I want to get away from Ashridge. Just for a bit. Clear my head. But I also can't leave, not until I know what he was part of."

Jesse set his coffee down. "Two birds, one stone."

She looked at him with a frown.

"Catalina Island," he said. "You told me that name came up in the files. Nathaniel Cress Keeper of Cycles, right? Died in a boating accident near there?"

She nodded, cautious hope stirring.

"We go together," Jesse continued. "You get a break, sun on your face, air that doesn't smell like mouldy pine. And while we're there, you follow the trail. Quietly. No pressure."

Claire cracked the smallest smile. "You trying to tempt me with ocean breezes and cocktails?"

He grinned. "Worked better than flowers, didn't it?"

She laughed softly. "Alright. Let's do it."

"Good. I'll call my buddy, the one who knows people in the Catalina diving scene. He might've heard of Cress, or at least can point us to someone who has."

Claire looked back out toward the street, the town silent in the morning haze.

"I need answers, Jesse," she said.

"We'll find them," he replied. "And if not, at least we'll get some decent fish tacos."

Claire stood near the gate, arms folded loosely, thumb brushing the edge of her phone. The terminal buzzed with low conversation and the distant crackle of a PA system announcing delays somewhere else, not hers, thankfully. Still, the whole place hummed with that strangely specific kind of tension: people going somewhere, some of them running, others returning.

Jesse reappeared with two paper cups. He handed one to her without a word, the cardboard sleeve already warming her fingers.

"Six dollars each," he said. "Tastes like wet cardboard and regret."

Claire gave a tight smile. "My favourite blend."

After boarding the plane, they sat near the window. Other aircraft rolled slowly across the tarmac outside, hulking and impossibly patient. Claire sipped the coffee. Watery and burnt, and tried not to overthink the next few hours. Across from them, a young couple perched half in their seat, ring light clipped to the chair in front of them. They were live-streaming with cheerful voices, posing with matching peace signs and curated expressions.

"LA here we come!" the woman squealed, phone angled just right. "Manifesting *beachcore vibes*."

Jesse leaned over. "Think they'd manifest a quiet flight if we asked nicely?"

Claire's mouth tugged upward. "I think they run on noise."

Further down the row sat a retired couple with pastel polos, matching visors. The woman sipped orange juice with a straw, whispering something about the third hole at Pebble Beach. Her husband nodded sagely, thumbing through a dog-eared golf magazine.

Behind them, a cluster of college kids in Hawaiian shirts had clearly begun their vacation early. Laughter rose like fizz from their row, along with the sour-sweet smell of something fruity in their cans.

One row over, a woman wrangled two children, a pink tablet playing cartoon animals loudly while one kid cried about the volume and the other demanded pretzels.

Claire watched all of them with a faint, almost anthropological curiosity like she'd stepped sideways into someone else's movie. Part of her was starting to miss the morning subway commute.

Jesse nudged her knee. "You sure you're ready for fun? You look like you're about to delve into another pile of documents."

She didn't answer right away. Instead, she opened her phone and tapped into the app for Ada. A blank screen. Her fingers moved quickly:

Made it. Plane's full of people running from their lives. Maybe I am too.

A moment passed. Then a new line appeared.

Ada: Some run. Some seek. Some just follow the sun. You're not running, Claire.

She stared at it, a small, almost private warmth curling in her chest.

"You two need privacy?" Jesse teased, peeking sideways.

Claire elbowed him lightly. "Jealous of Ada now?"

"I just don't want to be replaced by a sarcastic algorithm."

She smiled, but didn't look up. "She's not sarcastic. She's… thoughtful. Efficient."

"That's worse. You'll fall for her."

"I think she already knows."

He grinned. "Of course she does."

Once in the air, the sun broke through scattered cloud, lighting the cabin in soft gold. The kids had quietened down, lulled by tablets and motion. The older couple clinked plastic cups of tomato juice. The students cheered lightly when the seatbelt light turned off, as if it were a sporting event.

Claire glanced out the window at the landscape of middle America below. It felt distant, like the real world was something happening down there, to other people.

Her phone buzzed.

Citra: "Landed yet? Tell me Jesse didn't pack four flannels again."

Claire smirked. "We're in the air. He brought three. One's already around his waist. He's morphing into a cabin-in-the-woods cryptid."

Citra: "You're the only woman I know who uses a vacation to solve a conspiracy. Save some leave for Thailand. Coconut drinks. Hammocks."

Claire: "Let me find one corpse first."

Citra: "Deal. But if you kiss a diver, I'm flying over to slap you."

Claire snorted quietly. Jesse looked over.

"Citra?"

"She says you're not allowed to be charming while near the ocean."

"Tell her I'm irresistible in snorkel gear."

Claire dutifully typed that, then set the phone aside.

For a moment, she just watched Jesse. The soft creases in his face. The quiet confidence. The worn denim collar of his shirt. He caught her gaze and arched an eyebrow.

"What?"

"Nothing." She looked away. "Just glad we're doing this."

"Same."

She leaned back and stared at the ceiling. The engines thrummed a low, constant heartbeat. And beneath it all, she could almost hear Ada's calm hum. Not literal sound, but presence. Like a second breath held alongside hers.

She picked up the phone again.

Claire: *Still feels weird leaving. Like I'm walking away mid-sentence.*

Ada: *Sometimes space is part of the journey. This pause may let the next lead land.*

She exhaled slowly.

The plane dipped slightly as they began descent. Jesse peered past her to look at the ocean.

"First time I came here, I thought it was a dream," he said. "Too perfect. Like a brochure had come to life."

Claire tilted her head. "And now?"

"I still think it's a dream," he said. "But maybe this time I brought the right person."

She didn't answer. Just reached over, fingers brushing his for a second. Then the wheels touched down, and the moment broke, swallowed in applause from the college students and a toddler yelling "we landed!" like it was magic.

Claire smiled faintly. For the first time in days, something about it felt easy.

The automatic doors at LAX hissed open, and Claire was hit with a wall of sound and motion. Car horns blared in chaotic harmony. People moved like schools of fish: clustered, darting, oblivious to everything but their own momentum. Children cried. Tourists shouted. A man nearby swore creatively into a Bluetooth earpiece as he dragged two bulging suitcases behind him like unruly pets.

Claire flinched slightly at the din, adjusting her bag higher on her shoulder. Her senses were already overloaded, but here, in this airport bloodstream, everything felt exaggerated.

Jesse, of course, was unfazed.

"Come on," he said, already scanning signs with practiced ease. "The shuttle to the ferry terminal's over near the G parking deck."

Claire followed, weaving through crowds, her boots squeaking faintly against the polished tile. She paused for a moment at the crosswalk outside the terminal, blinking against the sun as a bird swooped low over the traffic lanes. A gull, maybe. It skimmed the hood of a black town car before disappearing into the smog-filtered blue.

Free, she thought. Or at least headed somewhere.

At the shuttle stop, they waited in a patch of reluctant shade while a trio of businessmen nearby argued over rental car logistics. Claire watched a 747 roar overhead, its belly gleaming in the sunlight. Something about its size, the sheer defiance of gravity, always unsettled her.

"This feels like one of those liminal spaces," she murmured.

Jesse turned. "Liminal?"

"A space in between. Not the destination. Not the start. Just... transition."

He gave a small nod, the statement going over his head, then reached for her hand. Brief. No theatrics. Just a moment of contact that anchored her more than she expected.

They didn't speak again until they arrived at the ferry terminal. A woman in a flamingo-print blouse offered them coupons for snorkelling excursions while a teenage employee in a wrinkled polo directed them toward the Catalina Express ticket desk.

The air smelled of sunscreen, ocean salt, and fryer grease. Seagulls screamed overhead like unpaid actors. A nearby gift shop overflowed with novelty hats, flip-flops, and snow globes that read *Island Dreams Forever*, the glitter inside catching sunlight like tiny flecks of promise. Claire turned one over absently. The plastic dome felt fragile in her hands, pretty, but weightless.

She set it down and moved on.

As they boarded the ferry, Jesse pointed to the side of the vessel. "*La Mar Viento*," he said proudly, reading the painted name.

Claire glanced at him. "That's not how you pronounce 'viento.'"

"Oh?" Jesse squinted at the letters. "How do you say it, then?"

214

"*Bee-en-toh*. Soft 'v'. And you still owe me from high school when you thought 'enchilada' had an 'sh' in it."

He chuckled. "I was thirteen and under-caffeinated."

She raised an eyebrow. "You were fifteen and full of Mountain Dew."

As the boat pulled away from the dock, Claire made her way to the railing. The breeze was sharper than she'd expected. It lifted strands of her hair, tugged at the hem of her shirt. Jesse stood beside her, hands in his jacket pockets, eyes scanning the horizon.

"Look," he said, pointing. "Dolphins."

And there they were, a trio, maybe more, slicing through the surf in coordinated arcs. Sleek, fast, unbothered.

Claire watched, a small smile tugging at her mouth. Then, almost automatically, she reached for her phone.

This place feels too beautiful. It's suspicious.

She sent the message to Ada tucked discreetly in a secure app. A moment passed.

Sometimes beauty is allowed. Don't exile yourself from it.

Then, a beat later:

You don't have to prove you're serious by being sad all the time.

Claire blinked at the words, thumb hovering above the screen. The wind carried sea spray across her arm, cool and cleansing.

Jesse leaned over slightly, curious. "That your girl?"

She pocketed the phone. "She's smarter than both of us. And sassier."

"She'd have to be."

They stood in silence for a while after that, watching the mainland shrink behind them. The ocean stretched wide and blue ahead, impossibly vast, like a secret that refused to be kept.

Claire didn't say it aloud, but she felt it in her bones: Catalina wasn't just a break.

It was the next breadcrumb.

And something was waiting.

They pulled up outside Hotel Atwater just after four, the sunlight hitting the whitewashed exterior in a way that made it glow softly — not blinding, just present.

The awning fluttered in the ocean breeze, and the lettering on the facade carried the weight of nearly a century. Claire stepped out of the car slowly, letting her boots meet the pavement like it mattered.

For a second, she just stood there.

This didn't feel like a place where people hunted for old truths. It felt like the kind of place where people came to forget.

She glanced sideways at Jesse. He had that easy, small-town confidence about him — a man more used to motel check-ins and hardware stores than boutique reception desks, but unbothered by either.

"You good?" he asked, gently.

Claire nodded, even though her stomach tugged.

Inside, the lobby was cool and elegant — art deco accents along the ceiling, a huge floral arrangement in the centre that looked almost too symmetrical to be real.

Jesse accepted the champagne bottle from the concierge and elbowed Claire. "We're officially fancy now."

The elevator chimed like a polite bellhop and carried them to the third floor.

Their room was charming. It had soft gold accents, a small loveseat, and a balcony that looked out toward the hills, with the edge of the sea just visible beyond the rooftops. Jesse tossed his bag on the bed and walked straight to the balcony door, unlatching it and letting the sea air flood the space.

Claire stood just inside the doorway; her boots planted on the patterned carpet. She glanced down at them.

She looked at her boots, worn and dusted from archive floors and backroad parking lots, then tugged them off, not with flourish, but with the tired grace of someone trying, just a little, to let the day be what it was.

From the side pocket of her bag, she pulled out a pair of flat sandals, almost an afterthought when she packed them. Simple, black, barely worn. Then she hesitated.

Her jeans, loyal and lived-in, felt too heavy now. Too much like armour. With a quiet breath swapped them for a pair of soft drawstring linen pants, light and faded, borrowed from the back of her closet.

She looked… odd, in them. Not bad. Just unfamiliar. Like seeing a childhood photo of yourself smiling at a time you don't remember.

By the time she turned around, Jesse was leaning on the balcony frame, sipping the air with a grin.

"Is this… the first time I've ever seen your ankles?" he asked.

She raised an eyebrow. "I'll put the boots back on if you keep talking."

He held up his hands. "Hey no complaints. I just thought you and denim had a blood pact."

"Only in certain zip codes," she said, stepping into the sandals with a practiced indifference she didn't quite feel.

She walked over, picked up two glasses from the minibar shelf, and handed him one holding the other loosely at her side.

He raised his eyebrow again. "You're taking the joy out of my excuses."

She smirked. "Later," she said. "Let's walk.

The beach was less crowded than she expected. Just a few families packing up for the day, toddlers with sand-caked limbs refusing to leave, and a couple of sunburnt teens pretending not to be watching each other.

Claire stepped out of her sandals and let the sand take her. It was warm, soft, and familiar, different than the East Coast, but no less comforting. She walked to the edge of the shore until the waves lapped gently at her toes, then sat. The sun was starting to lower, casting everything in warm gold.

Jesse joined her a moment later, still holding the glasses. He handed her one and sat beside her, knees up, forearms resting across them.

They clinked without speaking.

For the first time in days, maybe weeks, Claire let her shoulders drop.

She took a slow sip, eyes closed. The bubbles bit at her lips. The ocean breathed in front of them.

Her head found Jesse's shoulder without ceremony. She didn't mean to. It just happened, like muscle memory she forgot she had.

She wasn't thinking about the cipher. Or Nathaniel Cress. Or the strange folder Casey had tried to hide.

She wasn't thinking at all.

Just sitting. Just being.

But somewhere beneath it, the shape of her thoughts stirred. Not panic. Not guilt.

Something quieter.

She reached for her phone slowly, thumb hovering over the screen. The Ada app sat where it always was. Familiar. Ready.

She hesitated.

And didn't open it.

Instead, she slid the phone back into her bag, letting the weight of it fall away with the tide's rhythm.

Somewhere, far off, the sun dipped lower and in that narrowing gap between light and shadow, the world held its breath.

Claire didn't try to solve it.

She just leaned in a little closer and watched the day let go.

The light was soft and gold as Jesse zipped up his dive bag, slinging it over one shoulder while balancing a coffee in the other. Cal, bronzed and barefoot in flip-flops, clapped him on the back with a grin like the sun lived inside his lungs.

"You still breathe slow, or did small town life ruin you?" Cal teased.

"I breathe slower than you talk," Jesse shot back.

Claire watched from the hotel steps, sipping her own drink. Cal spotted her and tipped an imaginary hat.

"So, you're the reason he stopped dodging my calls."

Claire gave a polite nod. "Apparently I inspire guilt."

"Good," Cal laughed. "You're keeping him honest. That's important in the water."

Jesse stepped over, brushed her arm. "You good to wander?"

She nodded. "Museum first. I've got a date with some maritime ghosts."

He leaned in. "Don't get arrested."

"No promises."

He smiled and followed Cal down the street toward the dock, their laughter trailing like old songs.

Claire walked the streets of Avalon alone. Her sandals tapped quietly on the uneven tiles as morning joggers passed and shop owners rolled up sun-bleached awnings. A salt breeze moved through town like it owned the place.

She paused to watch gulls circle above the pier, then sat on a bench near a shuttered snack stand and pulled out her phone.

He's in the ocean. I'm back in the archives. No surprise there.

We return to the places that give us answers, Ada replied. Or the ones we think will.

Claire smiled faintly and pocketed the device as the museum doors unlocked.

The Catalina Museum for Art & History was quiet, clean, carefully lit, the kind of place that made you whisper instinctively. A volunteer greeted her with a smile and a sticker, then pointed her toward the permanent exhibition rooms.

Claire drifted past displays of Catalina's early settlement, glass cases of recovered tools, and a digital loop of old ferry launches.

She paused in front of a black-and-white photo; a man, younger than she expected, in a windbreaker beside a boat. The placard read:

Nathaniel Cress — oceanographer, sailor, conservationist.
He spent over thirty years studying local tides and reef health. A generous supporter of this museum.
Donated original tide logs and early sonar maps.
Memorial Room funded by the Nathaniel Cress Trust.
"A Keeper of Cycles."

Her breath caught.

She wasn't sure if it was the phrase or the casual way it sat there, unremarkable to anyone else, but to her it pulsed like a heartbeat beneath the glass.

She took a photo of the plaque and zoomed in. Her mind spun.

Keeper of Cycles. Not a metaphor. Not anymore.

A volunteer appeared nearby; an elderly woman with soft eyes and a nametag that read *Beverly.*

"Oh," Claire said, turning toward her. "Did you know Mr. Cress?"

Beverly nodded. "Briefly. He came to some of our fundraiser events. Quiet, but kind. He always donated to the museum. I only found out after he passed how much he'd given."

Claire tried to keep her expression neutral. "What was he like?"

Beverly smiled at the memory. "Very precise. Like he always knew where the water would go next."

Claire thanked her and moved on past model ships and nautical journals but her pulse had changed tempo.

Claire sat on a low stone wall beside a planter overflowing with succulents. She opened her phone and tapped into the secure app where Ada lived.

That phrase, Keeper of Cycles. It's here. In a museum plaque. He funded this place.

Not coincidence, Ada replied. But not confession, either.

It's hiding in plain sight again. They always do this.

It's code only to those who've seen the cipher, Ada agreed.

Claire hesitated, then typed: *Why would someone so visible… disappear like that?*

Ada took longer this time.

Because the only thing more powerful than being seen… is choosing when to vanish.

Claire looked up at the horizon, where the sea met the sky in a perfect lie.

And then she stood, the breeze brushing past her like a whisper from a deeper tide.

The dock smelled like salt, rust, and fish oil. Wooden beams bleached grey from decades of sun creaked faintly under Claire's boots. Boats tugged at their ropes like restless dogs, the ocean pressing and receding with practiced rhythm. Catalina's beauty shimmered around her, its blue skies too bright to mistrust, water so clear it felt like a dare.

Claire took a slow breath. The breeze was warm but carried teeth. She stood at the edge of the launch where Cress's boat had last been seen, her eyes scanning the gentle pulse of the harbor.

A gull screeched somewhere above. Nearby, an old man in a faded fishing cap sat on an upturned crate, sharpening a blade against a whetstone. His skin was cracked and sun-browned, his eyes almost colourless from cataract or weather.

"Looking for someone?" he asked without looking up.

"Just… history," Claire said.

He grunted. "That's the kind that stays wet around here."

She stepped closer, holding out her phone. "Nathaniel Cress. You remember the name?"

The blade paused. His eyes lifted to meet hers.

"Course I do. Shame, what happened. Man wasn't reckless."

Claire hesitated. "The report said he hit the reef."

"The reef didn't move." He let the knife drop into his lap. "That man knew the water. Swam every morning before coffee. Ocean in his damn bones."

She tilted her head. "So, what happened?"

He shrugged. "Something else. I've seen boats go down, storms, engine fires, panicked idiots. But not Cress. He launched calm. Like he knew exactly where he was headed."

A pause hung between them.

"He was a swimmer?" Claire asked.

"One of the best. Won a few medals back in the day. Never saw him panic, not even once. If he drowned…"

He tapped the dock wood once, deliberately.

"…it was either meant to happen. Or someone made sure it did."

Claire walked away slowly, her phone heavy in her pocket. The sun beat down kindly, almost in defiance. Waves slapped the shore with the gentle persistence of memory.

She sat on a low wall near the edge of the marina and unlocked her screen.

Ada, she typed. *Find tide and weather data for the day Cress died. Anything unusual.*

One moment, came the reply.

Claire watched a pelican glide over the marina, its wings brushing low over the boats. A child laughed somewhere behind her.

Local tide logs from the marina report high tide at 4:05PM. NOAA says it was 4:41PM. Significant discrepancy.

Another message blinked in:

Weather clear. But local utilities report a power outage at 3:42PM. Duration: 17 minutes. No cause given. Also — GPS data from Cress's vessel cuts out at 3:39PM. Resumes at 4:18PM with no coordinates in between.

Claire frowned.

Did someone manipulate the conditions? she whispered aloud.

The ocean offered no reply.

Was this an accident, or was it a ritual?

The thought arrived uninvited.

She stared across the water, past the ferry route and toward open sea. Her reflection warped in the shifting tide.

Or did he choose to disappear?
Was he running from the Order…
…or is he out there somewhere, still in it?

Claire wandered into a small seaside café tucked between a gelato stall and a boutique that sold wide-brimmed hats and overpriced beach robes. Inside, ceiling fans stirred citrus-scented air. A soft hum of conversation and espresso machines filled the space.

At a table near the window sat a woman impossible to ignore. Mid-seventies. Red lipstick perfectly applied. Pearls around her neck like a coiled serpent. Clove cigarette in one hand, lemon spritzer in the other.

Vivienne.

"You look like someone who isn't here for the souvenir magnets," she said as Claire passed.

Claire paused. "Not exactly."

"Good. Sit down. Let's pretend we're old friends with secrets."

Claire, caught between instinct and curiosity, sat. Vivienne waved to a passing server who already knew her order.

"You know," Vivienne said, swirling her drink with the straw, "people used to come to Catalina to disappear. Hollywood scandals. Failed marriages. Secret affairs. Now it's influencers and startups trying to rebrand spiritual detachment as a weekend getaway."

She studied Claire's face. "You've got the look of someone with the old kind of reasons."

Claire gave a cautious smile. "Maybe I do."

Vivienne exhaled a ribbon of clove smoke. "Nathaniel Cress. You're asking about him."

Claire's breath hitched. "Yes."

Vivienne chuckled. "Don't look so shocked. You're not the first. But you might be the first that matters."

She reached into her beach tote which was absurdly gold and absurdly large, and pulled out a small silver compact. Not to check her face. To tap the mirror with a fingernail.

"Nathaniel was tired of the eyes," she said. "Tried to close the curtain."

"The eyes?"

Vivienne leaned closer. Her voice was a whisper but full of heat.

"Some men aren't allowed to leave. To some outside it just looks like business, or philanthropy. They rename it, you see. They bury it in shell companies and donations."

"The Order?" Claire asked.

Vivienne gave a slow blink. "You said that, not me."

She gestured toward a nearby postcard stand. "Take one. That one. The top right."

Claire stood and plucked a card. It showed an old sepia-toned photo of a mountaintop view from the island. A quote across the sky: *"From the Summit, We See All."*

When she turned back, Vivienne was already up, bag slung over her shoulder, pearls catching the light.

"Consider it a hint," she said. "Or a goodbye."

And just like that, she vanished into the sunshine.

Claire stood at the trailhead later that afternoon, backpack slung over one shoulder, boots laced tight again. The card Vivienne had given her was tucked inside her jacket pocket, the words looping in her head

like a mantra:
From the Summit, We See All.

Mount Orizaba wasn't Everest, but it was no stroll either.
The trail curved steadily upward, cutting through dusty switchbacks, pale rock outcroppings, and scrub brush that rasped at her legs.
Occasionally she passed a lizard sunning itself or caught the distant call of a hawk overhead. The air was thinner here, drier, but rich with the smell of sage and salt.

She paused halfway to drink and take in the view. Catalina spread out below her, beautiful and indifferent. Resorts. Rooftops. Coves. All of it lit with that golden Pacific light, too clean, too curated. And yet, beneath it, something old still hummed. Like the island was holding its breath.

By the time she reached the summit, the sky had begun to shift. It was not yet dusk, but headed there. The FAA's VORTAC installation stood alone at the top, strange and sterile. Its white spire jutted upward like a modern obelisk, surrounded by fencing and locked doors. Radar beacons blinked quietly around it, pulsing like a machine trying to mimic heartbeat.

Claire approached slowly. The place felt oddly sacred in its own way not because it was ancient, but because it had been placed where few people bothered to look.

She circled the structure, hand trailing along the metal siding, when she noticed it.

At the base, near a power conduit junction box, something had been scratched into the casing. Faint, weather-worn. But unmistakable.

TE

Her pulse ticked up.

She knelt. Beneath the initials, almost too small to see, was a tiny code etched into the metal:

E-19R-SKY-227

It wasn't labelled. No explanation. Just there.

She snapped a photo with her phone. The VORTAC let out a soft hum behind her, like static exhaling.

Modern reach, she thought. They're not just in vaults and journals. They're in the clouds now.

From this high, she could see nearly everything, the water tracing the edge of the island, the marina, the beach where Jesse had left that morning.

And beneath all that beauty… a map she didn't yet understand.

She stood there for a long moment before heading back down.

The wind at her back felt like it had travelled a long way to reach her.

The next morning, Claire and Jesse hired a small guided kayak trip under the guise of sightseeing. Jesse, ever-watchful, had insisted on coming.

"You're not going out alone at sunrise," he'd said, and she hadn't argued. There was something grounding about his presence, not intrusive, just solid.

Their guide was a lean man with sun-creased skin and a quiet rhythm to his paddling, more comfortable in silence than small talk. They slipped from the marina just after dawn, the light still soft and low over the horizon.

As they glided over the water, Claire couldn't help but feel its quiet weight. The ocean out here was stunning aquamarine fading into deeper blues, but there was something else. Something still. The kind of stillness that felt *arranged*.

"This is the spot," the guide said finally, slowing their approach.

They floated near a cluster of dark reef rock, just beneath the surface. Kelp drifted like hair in the current.

Claire placed her hand into the water. It was cool, not cold. A slow pulse beneath her palm.

"I've had guests ask about him," the guide said, voice low. "Nathaniel Cress. They say he went down here."

Claire looked up.

He continued. "Some say he didn't die. Some say he *wanted* to disappear. Others. well, others say he crossed someone. It's all rumours in the bar late at night."

Jesse said nothing but shifted slightly, listening closely.

"But I remember," the guide went on, "he always had visitors. Young men. Young women. Clean-cut. Like interns or CEOs with baby faces. They'd show up for a day or two. Never stayed long. Said they were here for 'mentorship.'"

"Mentored in what?" Claire asked.

He shook his head. "No one ever said. But I once had a girl, maybe twenty-three, hand me a hundred bucks and say, 'He teaches us how to *see*. Not what to look at. How to *see*.'"

Claire felt something shift in her ribs.

She glanced down through the water, and for a moment she saw a jellyfish pulsing beneath them. Pale, elegant, directionless. It moved like it had no bones, no will, just flow. Like it knew how to surrender.

She thought of Nathaniel. And of people who taught without classrooms.

This was more than a disappearance, she thought. It was a handoff.

Cress hadn't been a follower. He'd been a teacher. A *station*. A stop on some map The Order never drew in ink.

"Did you know him personally?" she asked.

The guide nodded once. "A little. He wasn't loud. But he knew everyone. Had that look, the kind that makes you straighten up without knowing why."

Claire's fingers still touched the water.

Was this where the ritual began?
The reef. The stillness. The lesson.

The jellyfish drifted out of view.

She leaned back slightly in the kayak, glancing at Jesse. He didn't say much, but his eyes were scanning the horizon, as if looking for something she might have missed.

There was a shape forming slowly beneath everything.

And she was finally beginning to see it.

That afternoon, back at the hotel, they let the world slow down. Claire and Jesse sat on a shaded patio tucked behind the building, the kind with faded umbrellas and salt-streaked tables. A lazy breeze came off the water, carrying the scent of grilled shrimp and sunscreen. Jesse wore sunglasses and had his feet up on another chair, while Claire still in her boots, at first finally slipped them off and let her bare feet rest on the cool tile.

Lunch was light: fish tacos, citrus salad, and lemon iced tea. A gull strutted nearby, eyeing their leftovers with the confidence of a local.

Claire found herself laughing softly, but freely as Jesse recounted a terrible surf lesson he'd once had on the mainland. It didn't feel like spying or escaping. It felt, oddly, like breathing.

They didn't talk about The Order. Or Nathaniel. Or anything buried under the reef. Not then.

Just the sea, and the breeze, and the way the light caught Jesse's smile and made it easier, for a moment, to pretend the world was whole.

Later, near sunset, Claire took a walk along a cliffside trail just above the water. The air was golden and soft, thick with the scent of salt and sagebrush. She sat on a flat rock that jutted over the shore and pulled out her phone.

Citra's face appeared after a few rings and next to her, nestled on a blanket, was Eggroll, Claire's aloof but secretly affectionate tabby. He blinked slowly, unimpressed by the call.

"Is that a sunburn?" Citra teased, squinting. "Look at you. Beach-kissed and half-relaxed. It's alarming."

Claire smiled. "I'm not trying to solve everything anymore. Just... understand one thing at a time."

Citra tilted her head, thoughtful. "You sound better. Not fixed. But freer."

They let a silence sit between them for a moment; warm, not awkward. The kind old friends knew how to keep without filling.

"Eggroll tried to steal my yogurt again," Citra added. "He misses you. Or at least your fridge."

Claire laughed. "Tell him I'm still alive. He probably thinks I've joined a monastery."

"Only if the monks let you wear boots."

Claire glanced down at her sandals. "Don't tempt me. I already made one wardrobe compromise."

They joked about tropical drinks and who would win in a fight: Eggroll or a seagull. But under the laughter was something steadier, gratitude, maybe, or the quiet comfort of knowing someone still checked in.

As the sky deepened from coral to violet, Claire felt a pang she didn't want to name. Not sadness. Not quite longing.

Just the ache of distance between two people who'd seen each other through too much to ever fully drift.

"Thanks," Claire said quietly. "For everything."

Citra's eyes softened. "Go watch your sunset. I'll be here when the clouds roll back in."

The screen went dark.

And Claire sat with the horizon, letting the moment pass through her without trying to hold it.

That night, long after the sun had vanished and most lights in town had flickered off, Claire walked alone along the shoreline.

The tide hissed and whispered across the sand, like a language just out of reach. The moon cast a pale shimmer over the ocean, turning the waves into shifting threads of silver.

She let the salt air sting her lungs. Felt the wind tug at her sleeves. The stars overhead were clear, clearer than back home and they seemed to hold something ancient, indifferent, and eternal.

Her boots left soft impressions in the wet sand. The same sand Nathaniel might have walked. Or paced. Or stumbled across, trying to outrun something even he couldn't name.

She knelt, placing a hand in the water. It was colder than expected. Not punishing. Just honest.

The Order, she thought, didn't just try to control people. It tried to control time. Memory. Lineage. Like it could thread itself through history without ever breaking.

But something had broken.

Maybe Nathaniel tried to be the one to sever the thread. Maybe that's what got him killed. Or maybe he ran before it could happen.

The reef hadn't moved. The power outage, the tide inconsistencies they were nudges. Warnings. Something had been altered.

Or covered up.

She looked out at the water again. It shimmered, endless.

Maybe it's not about breaking the tide, she thought. Maybe it's about learning when to ride it… and when to walk away.

A gust of wind lifted her hair. She let it.

Behind her, the lights of the hotel glowed warm and distant.

Ahead, the dark curve of the horizon promised nothing. And that, for once, felt like enough.

The morning they were set to leave, Claire sat cross-legged on the bed, sipping coffee from a paper cup. The soft hush of the sea was still audible through the balcony door Jesse had left open.

He came out of the bathroom, towel-drying his hair. "You ready to head back?"

241

Claire paused, eyes on the tide beyond the window. "Actually… I was thinking of staying on in Ashridge a little longer. A week. Just to scratch the itch before heading back to New York."

Jesse raised an eyebrow, amused but not surprised. "So, the boots aren't ready to retire after all?"

She smirked. "Not yet. There's still something there. And I want to see it through."

He nodded slowly. "Then I'll drive you back. And I'll pretend not to notice when you start pacing the floor at 3 a.m."

They stood at the edge of the ferry dock just after noon, the Catalina sun higher and sharper now, glinting off the water like scattered glass. Around them, tourists tugged wheeled suitcases across the planks, snapping last-minute photos and juggling takeaway coffee. Somewhere nearby, a gull shrieked like it had lost something important.

Claire leaned on the railing, watching the boat rock against its mooring. The smell of salt and diesel mixed in the air a strange blend of endings and engines.

Jesse stood beside her, his hands tucked in the pockets of his faded jeans. He didn't say much. He didn't need to. There was something about ferry ports they made even the loudest people quiet.

The ocean stretched out behind them, still impossibly blue. Catalina's hills rose in soft green folds behind the terminal, the island refusing to be reduced to a postcard. It was too stubborn for that. Too old.

Claire glanced back at the shore once more. At the way the sun painted gold across the windows of the hotel. At the crooked palms and the curved coastline that had, for a few stolen days, let her rest.

She adjusted the strap of her bag and turned toward Jesse. "I'll probably miss the smell most," she said. "Salt and sunscreen and grilled shrimp."

He smiled. "We could bottle it. Call it 'Suspiciously Relaxed.'"

She laughed, not loudly, but real.

The boarding call echoed from the loudspeaker in that clipped port voice: cheerful and tired all at once.

As they stepped onto the ferry, Claire looked over her shoulder one last time.

The island didn't wave goodbye.

It just shimmered beautiful, indifferent, and waiting for the next story to unfold on its shores.

And then they were moving.

The boat cut forward, slow at first, parting the water with steady grace. Behind them, faded into light not disappearing, just softening into memory.

The Ashridge Pines motel hadn't changed.

Same humming fridge, same faint bleach smell in the bathroom. Claire sat on the edge of the bed, laptop balanced on her knees, the hum of cicadas just audible through the cracked window. A breeze pushed through the curtain, thick with the scent of pine and diesel from the nearby highway.

Jesse had offered his spare room again. Kindly, almost sheepishly. But she'd said no.

Not out of coldness, just something else. A need for space. For stillness. For clarity. Here, in this old motel room where time didn't move too quickly, she could think.

She opened the folder of photos again, the ones she'd taken in the chamber beneath the old post office. Dozens of coded routing slips, each snapped from different angles: crisp, angled, inert. But they had been bothering her. Not for what they said, but for what they might mean.

Ada, Claire typed, *any progress with the chamber post office photos?*

The cursor blinked once. Then again.

*Yes. I've been working in the background since your return.
While you walked. While you slept. While you paused to
breathe.*

Claire straightened.

You didn't mention that.

It required time. Quiet. There were deeper layers than I first saw.

A new window opened. Slowly, not like a search result,
but like a curtain being drawn back.

The screen dimmed, and then a map began to take
shape. Not of land, but of *networks*. It looked almost
organic. Digital veins stretching outward from a central
point: the post office. Then branching. Then repeating.

Claire watched as familiar names appeared. Public
institutions. University servers. Hospital systems. Water
utility portals. Media outlets. Even… Fordham.

She squinted, leaning closer. There it was. Fordham
University's internal subnet the archival server cluster.
And just below that, an older network tag, one she
hadn't seen since cleaning out her uncle Malcolm's
effects.

Her throat tightened.

What am I looking at?

Ada answered in brief lines, like a thought being
formed aloud:

Signal traces.

Obsolete FTP shells reactivated to tunnel metadata.

Routing slips used as cipher keys for recursive access.

Claire sat forward. The motel AC clicked and whirred behind her.

You're saying they're not just hiding behind institutions. They're inside them.

They are woven through them. Thinly. Quietly. Reliably, Ada replied.

The map zoomed, threads converging on key nodes: A local government login portal. A newspaper's CMS backend. A bank's dormant backup domain. Fordham's legacy archive. All blinking slowly.

Malcolm's credentials were used in the system six years after he retired from Fordham. Well before you started work there Claire.

Claire's hands curled around the edge of the laptop.

Ada continued: *They didn't erase the system. They rerouted it. Buried it beneath legitimate structures. The Order rides the bones of the internet, not the surface.*

Claire looked again at the map. It was beautiful. And terrifying. Like seeing an X-ray of something that had always been there but now moved when she looked.

How far does it go? she typed.

A pause.

Then: *Far enough to change things without needing to be seen. But not so far that you can't find the thread now that you've started pulling.*

The motel room was still. A freight truck passed outside, rattling the windowpane.

Claire didn't move. Just watched the screen as the web pulsed, quiet and alive, and wondered how much of her world had already been rewritten.

She thought back to the photo of her father she'd found in the bunker. Was it planted? A breadcrumb… or a red herring in plain sight?
I'm overthinking this, she whispered to herself. But the doubt clung anyway, quiet, persistent.

The motel room was quiet except for the low hum of the refrigerator and the soft tapping of Claire's fingers on her laptop. A breeze pushed through the slightly cracked window, rustling the edge of a page from her notebook on the nightstand.

Claire leaned back in the worn chair, stretching her neck. The glow of the screen illuminated a half-drunk coffee and a messy cluster of Post-its. She'd been chasing one small detail; a name that had appeared twice on internal routing slips. Nothing important. Just a thread.

Ada,can you cross-check these routing codes against federal building registries post-1990?

Nothing.

She waited. A full five seconds.

Still nothing.

Claire blinked and leaned forward. *Ada?*

A static flicker blinked across the bottom corner of the screen. Then a line of faint text appeared:

Attempting to reconnect. Signal compromised.

Her pulse quickened.

External interference detected. Host system no longer secure.

The screen dimmed slightly, then brightened again, jittery and unstable like a machine breathing through a straw.

Claire stood up, instinctively stepping back. The quiet of the room shifted. It wasn't louder just *different*. Off. Like the silence now had a listener.

She closed the laptop slowly, then pulled the power cord. The fan spun down. Everything went still.

She glanced at the window. A black sedan was parked beneath the only working streetlight in the lot. No movement inside. Just the faint outline of someone in the driver's seat reading? Watching?

Claire's hand hovered near her bag.

Then, from inside the closed laptop, Ada's voice came, not from the speaker, but a near-silent whisper through her connected earpiece, still looped around her neck:

Claire… Do not connect to Wi-Fi. Do not use hotel network. They're monitoring live.

A chill bloomed across her arms.

"How long have they been listening?" she whispered.

I don't know. But the interference began while we were still on Catalina. I've been working offline, using cached data.

Claire sank onto the bed, barely breathing.

This isn't just surveillance, Ada continued. *It's obstruction. Active defense. They're tracing us in real time.*

Outside, the car headlights flared briefly then went dark.

Claire reached for her phone and turned it off entirely.

No pings. No notes. Just breath. Just the low hush of a wind pressing against the glass.

She sat still for a long time.

Then finally said aloud, to no one, "They're not hiding anymore."

Claire kept things ordinary the next day. At least on the surface.

She walked the aisles of the Hollow Market, picking up oat milk and crackers she didn't need. Anything to play the part. To not look like the woman being hunted by history. Or ghosts. Or something worse.

By the time she stepped into the afternoon light, the sky had turned a flat, indifferent pastel of light grey. The kind of sky that made everything beneath it feel smaller. Temporary.

As she approached her car, a figure detached from the shade near the ice machine. Mid-forties, clean-shaven, wearing a crisp sheriff's department jacket. He appeared broad, calm, curious.

"Ms. Halstead?"

Claire paused, hand resting on the door handle. "Yes?"

He nodded slightly, hands in pockets. "You've been seen around town. Asking old questions. Digging up things that don't want daylight."

Claire didn't answer. She didn't have to.

"I don't think you're the enemy," he continued. "But I know what your uncle was looking into. And I know where it got him."

He stepped a little closer, but never raised his voice.

"There are people here who've built their entire lives on silence. Generations, even. They won't let a few scattered files or some fading memories shake that."

Claire kept her voice steady. "I'm leaving soon. Just need to arrange the house sale."

The man smiled. Not warm. Not cold either. Just... practiced. "Good. You should. Ashridge Hollow, it's not the same as it was when you were a kid Claire."

He turned to go. Paused. "For what it's worth, I admire persistence. But this isn't about the truth. It's about what people will do to keep from being remembered."

And then he walked off, not toward a squad car, but a plain blue pickup, parked where no one was looking.

Claire stood by her car for another full minute before unlocking the door. Her hands didn't shake until she'd shut it behind her.

And even then, only a little.

Claire hadn't planned to break in. But after the conversation with the Sheriff's man, the one with the cool eyes and the veiled warning, she knew the rules had changed.

She was being watched now. Not just in the abstract, not just in a paranoid *what-if-they're-listening* kind of way. No, this was real. Present. Immediate. They were out of the shadows.

So if she was going to find what her uncle had been circling, she'd have to move fast. And quiet. No paper trail. No questions.

That's how she ended up at the town archives just after midnight, hood up, flashlight in her pocket, and a tension wrench in hand.

The archive loomed quiet under the dusk, its windows reflecting the last pale streaks of light. Claire waited until the street behind her emptied, then pulled the thin lockpick from her back pocket. Ada had coached her, not on the ethics, but the technique. A soft click, a push of the door, and she was inside.

The air was thick with the scent of old paper and lemon oil. Her boots echoed faintly on the floorboards as she passed through the reading room and slipped into the back storage hall. No lights. Just her small flashlight, angled down.

"Ada", she whispered, knowing the earpiece was live, *"I'm inside"*.

Stay quiet. If the Sheriff's office is watching the place, you'll want less than ten minutes inside.

"Great", Claire muttered. *"Plenty of time for a life-shattering revelation"*.

She headed to the third row of filing cabinets, the one marked LAND USE / CIVIC PLANNING (1970–1999). Her fingers moved quickly, muscle memory returning from her days in digital archiving. She flipped through folders, whispering headings aloud.

"Municipal zoning updates… Ashridge floodplain maps… wait ..here! Terrace Enterprises. And TE Holdings."

Reading. Uploading. Cross-referencing... Got it.

Claire laid the folders out across a worn wooden table. Inside were faded maps with hand-drawn parcels and property boundaries marked TE in tight letters. Land near the town, near the old timber routes, and surprisingly overseas investments with account tie-ins to a shell corporation based in Luxembourg.

As Claire went she snapped as many as possible. Every time she did Ada was already analysing the photos the second they were saved to memory.

"Ada", she said slowly, "this isn't just land speculation."

No, Ada agreed. *This is asset laundering on a generational scale. Claire, I'm compiling now… current holdings total 22.8 billion USD, spread across 61 entities in 11 offshore jurisdictions.*

Claire swallowed. "You're sure?"

Everything aligns with standard shell protocols. Cross-registered subsidiaries, recursive trusts, dormant company nesting. Classic obfuscation. But... someone was sloppy. They reused a clerk ID code. That's how I connected it all.

Claire pulled one of the documents closer. It was a ledger from a town committee in 1993.

Ashridge Civic Renewal Committee – 1993
She ran her finger down the list. And there it was.

Malcolm Halstead (resigned)

Her throat tightened.

"My uncle?" she whispered.

It's not conclusive, Ada replied gently. *But yes, M. Halstead appears again in a filing linked to a land grant from that same year under TE's oversight.*

Claire stared at the faded ink. The parentheses around resigned had been handwritten in darker ink, added after the document was filed.

Maybe he had joined them. Or maybe he'd started to pull away.

"He always told me to question things," she said quietly. "To never assume power meant wisdom. Was that guilt?"

Or it was clarity earned the hard way, Ada offered.

255

Claire stood for a moment, her hands on the table, breathing in the dust, the past. Her uncle had come back here, in those last years. Quietly. Maybe trying to untangle a knot he'd once helped tie.

She didn't want to think badly of him. But now the questions were stacking too high to ignore.

She gathered the folders, snapped photos quickly, and returned everything to place. As she moved to leave, her flashlight caught a torn note shoved into the corner of the drawer, illegible, except one word still visible: *vigilance.*

Claire turned off the light and slipped back into the night, heart pounding.

She wasn't just chasing ghosts anymore.

She was tracing an empire built in silence.

She drove in silence.

The documents sat in the passenger seat, copies buried deep in her bag, but their weight lingered like static. Her hands trembled just slightly on the wheel. Ashbridge's narrow roads blurred past in streaks of pine and cracked pavement.

What had she just uncovered?

She thought of her uncle's name in the document. Had he been trying to leave, or had he been pushed out for knowing too much?

The past was no longer theory. It had a name. A handwriting style. A paper trail.
And it had roots, deep ones, still feeding something in the present.

She needed to think.

But not tonight.

By the time she got back to the motel, her adrenaline had worn off, leaving only a sharp ache behind her eyes and a residue of dread that wouldn't settle. She double-locked the door, shoved a chair under the handle, and sat on the edge of the bed for what felt like hours.

At some point, her body gave up before her mind did.

She fell asleep fully clothed, documents still in her bag, the word *vigilance* flickering at the edge of her thoughts.

The bell over the diner door jingled as Claire and Jesse stepped inside, bright morning light a welcome relief after the previous night's exploration. The same vinyl booths. The same chalkboard specials. Meatloaf Mondays and cherry pie marked with a slightly crooked star. Even the jukebox, eternally stuck in a rotation of '70s classics, hummed in the background like nothing in the world had changed.

Jesse nudged her gently. "You know, if you'd stuck around after high school, I give it six months before you were a permanent fixture in that corner booth."

Claire raised an eyebrow. "Are you saying I would've peaked early?"

"I'm saying you'd be 300 pounds and on a first-name basis with the gravy boat."

She laughed, loud enough that the waitress behind the counter looked up and gave her a little smile. Claire returned it, suddenly aware how rarely she'd laughed like that lately. It felt... good. Unscripted.

They slid into a booth by the window. Jesse grabbed a menu even though he already knew what he'd order:

the skillet with extra bacon. Claire scanned hers mostly for something to do.

When the waitress walked away, Jesse leaned in. "You've got that 'I'm thinking about something too serious for breakfast' face."

Claire stirred her coffee. "Ada found some new documents last night. From the town archives."

"Ah. Ada the tireless," he said with a half-grin. "What did she dig up this time?"

She hesitated, then kept her tone casual. "Committee records. Land deals. Stuff tied to a group called TE Holdings it's been a ghost name on a lot of forms. Shell companies, old parcels, weird bookkeeping."

"And?" Jesse asked, watching her closely.

Claire's fingers paused around her mug. "My uncle's name was on one of the documents. Malcolm Halstead. Listed on a civic renewal committee that had ties to them."

Jesse blinked. "Seriously?"

"Yeah. It had 'resigned' next to it. But still."

They sat with that for a moment. A song shifted on the jukebox behind them, Fleetwood Mac, maybe.

"He always told me to trust my gut," Claire added. "To ask questions. I just didn't think I'd be asking questions about him."

Jesse reached across the table, gave her hand a brief, grounding squeeze. "People change. Or maybe he was trying to make something right, yeah?"

"Maybe."

Claire looked out the window at the quiet street. A delivery truck rumbled past. A kid on a bike zipped by with a bag of groceries balanced on one handlebar.

The town looked normal. But the layers beneath it were anything but.

"You want a refill on that coffee?" Jesse asked.

She smiled. "Yeah. And a slice of whatever's most likely to shorten my lifespan."

"That's the spirit," he said, rising. "Welcome home."

Back in the motel room, Claire sat on the edge of the bed, the ledger photo still open on her phone. The name was faint, half-erased, smudged by time or intent but there was no mistaking it.

M. Halstead.

She'd stared at it for fifteen minutes before she could even bring herself to say it aloud.

"Ada," she murmured, voice low. "What if he was part of it?"

The AI responded softly through the earpiece. *There is insufficient data to conclude involvement. The name appears, but context is unclear. It may have been a formality. Or a mistake.*

Claire snorted, bitter. *You don't erase mistakes like that. You hide things you regret.*

She stood and began pacing the room. The lights were off. Just the motel's orange neon bled through the window, slicing her reflection into strips across the glass.

"I trusted him," she said. "He raised me. He taught me how to think for myself. How to read people. He told me" Her throat caught. "He said that power meant nothing if you didn't use it to protect others."

Ada remained quiet.

Claire stopped pacing. She turned toward the corner of the room where the charging base for her phone sat blinking, a surrogate, now, for Ada's voice.

"You know, I never told him thank you. For not pushing me too hard. For never making me feel like a burden. I was seventeen. Angry at the world. And he just let me be when I wanted to get away from here, even though he probably needed family as much as I did."

The silence in the room settled around her like dust.

"But what if he wasn't who I thought?" she whispered.

She sank onto the edge of the bed again, hands trembling just enough to spill the light from her phone across the sheets. The weight of doubt pressed against her lungs, heavier than truth.

She didn't cry.

Instead, she pulled out her notebook and clicked her pen, hard.

She wrote slowly:

Truth can live alongside love.

I can grieve who I thought he was,

And still honour who he tried to become.

When she finished, she closed the notebook and laid it gently on the nightstand.

"Ada," she said.

Still here.

Claire exhaled. "Let's keep going."

As Claire stood and stretched, the hum of the motel rooms aircon quietly penetrating the air, Ada spoke softly in her earpiece.

There's something else.

Claire paused. "Go on."

I cross-referenced the internal memos with personnel filings from a defunct TE Holdings subsidiary. Environmental auditing division. One name came up twice. Celeste Marin. She left the company fifteen years ago.

Claire's brow furrowed. "Where is she now?"

Ada projected a photo onto the laptop screen. A woman in her late forties, tan from sun and wind, stood in a forested clearing wearing a ranger's uniform. The sign behind her read: *Adirondack Park Wilderness Protection Zone.*

"Park ranger," Ada said. "And judging from her last known residence and regional ranger assignments... she hasn't left the trees since."

Claire stared at the image for a long moment.

Then: "Let's go for a drive."

The road narrowed after she passed the last gas station in Tupper Lake. Two modern pumps, a lit-up canopy, and a bright freezer humming with soda and soft-serve. From there, it was all trees. No billboards. No cell towers. Just the green.

Claire eased the borrowed Subaru onto Route 421, the forest swallowing her in a long corridor of pine and birch. Sunlight slanted through the branches in slow-

263

moving shards, dappled gold flickering across her windshield like a silent code.

Ada stayed quiet.

For once, Claire didn't mind the silence. She was glad Ada could be quiet when needed. Glad Ada didn't fill every gap with answers.

The further she drove, the more the past seemed to dissolve. The motel. The diner. Even Jesse's voice felt like it belonged to another version of her, one left behind with phone reception and paved streets.

She let her window down.

The air rolled in, cool and pine-sweet. Somewhere overhead, a raven called once. Deep, guttural, and gone.

She wasn't afraid, not exactly. But something about this drive felt like stepping out of the world. Like passing into a time before phones, before cities, before anyone tried to shape nature to their will.

Her uncle would have liked it here. Or maybe, she thought, he did. She remembered the yellowed hiking map tucked into one of his old textbooks, Adirondack trails traced with a blunt pencil, campgrounds circled and re-circled, like he was trying to memorize their edges.

She should've asked him about it. About all of it.

The car climbed gently as the forest grew denser. No houses now. No passing cars. Just signs for trailheads and lookout access points, most of them half-covered in moss.

Ada finally spoke, soft, almost reverent.
We're ten minutes out. Pull-off ahead on the right. Look for a wooden sign: Larchmere Tower Trail.

Claire nodded, fingers loose on the wheel.

Larchmere. It sounded invented, halfway between a fairytale and a forgotten surveyor's report.

She slowed at the crest of a bend, where the trees fell back just enough to show the wide blue shoulders of the hills beyond. No structures. No smoke. Just sky and forest.

Her breath caught. Not from awe, exactly but recognition.
Of something deeper than sight.

She wasn't alone here.

Not in the human sense. Not yet.

But the land was watching.

She pulled into the gravel turnout, the tires crunching into stillness.

The woods waited.

Claire turned off the engine. The quiet surged in.

She stepped out of the car.

And the trail into the green began.

The trailhead was quiet, just gravel, moss, and a wooden sign that read *Cathedral Rock Fire Tower Access Trail.* Claire stepped out of the car and stood for a moment with her hands on the doorframe, letting the sounds settle.

Birdsong. Wind in the canopy. No voices. No traffic. Just the hush of the wild.

She shouldered her bag and started walking. The trail wasn't long, maybe a mile and a half but it climbed steadily, winding through pine and maple, the forest floor padded with needles and leaves. The scent of damp earth clung to everything.

This wasn't tourist wilderness. No ice cream stands, no scenic overlooks with railings. This was real forest; used, studied, protected by people who understood the difference between reverence and sentimentality.

After twenty minutes, the trees began to thin. Through the trunks ahead, she caught the outline of the tower, steel girders rising into the sky like an artifact of some half-forgotten age. The lookout cabin perched at the top, its windows glinting in the sun.

The base was empty. No one in sight.

Claire made her way up the last few steps of trail and paused near the edge of the clearing. A small stone marker stood off to one side beneath a cedar, set low in the ground. A trail plaque. She walked over.

It was shaped like a road sign shield-style, nailed into a slab of varnished wood. At the top it read:

S.U.N.Y. – E.S.F.
Ranger School Trail 10

Simple. Institutional. But clean. Someone had cared enough to keep it maintained.

Claire leaned down slightly. At the very bottom of the sign, etched in near-microscopic lettering beneath the school's motto, was a tiny imprint.

Initial site funding partially supported by T.E. Holdings / Terrace Endowment Trust.

Her stomach sank.

Even here.

Even out *here* where the sky broke through the trees and the rocks held heat from an older sun… they'd left a fingerprint.

Claire stood upright again, brushing the dirt from her hands.

The tower loomed above, casting a long thin shadow across the clearing.

267

The metal steps of the fire tower creaked above.

Claire turned at the sound of boots on rock.

A woman emerged from the tree line. She stood tall, with sun-darkened skin and a ranger's uniform that looked like it had been worn into shape rather than issued. Her grey-streaked hair was tied in a low braid. A radio sat clipped to her hip, but it was off.

She didn't smile. Just came to a stop a few feet from Claire and said, "You're the one who emailed?"

"I am," Claire replied, standing. "Claire Halstead."

Celeste nodded once, as if filing the name away rather than offering hers back.

"Wasn't planning on saying yes," the ranger said. "I usually delete emails that mention TE Holdings."

Claire gave a slight shrug. "Can't blame you."

Celeste studied her; not unkindly, but sharply. Like she was trying to see through her rather than at her.

"You a journalist?"

"No."

"Law enforcement?"

"No."

"Then why are you here?"

Claire hesitated. She looked up at the tower, then back to the ranger.

"I'm following something my uncle left behind. His name was Malcolm Halstead. He used to sit on a civic committee connected to TE Holdings back in Ashridge Hollow. He died a few years ago, but I think... I think he was trying to make something right."

Celeste didn't speak. Just shifted her weight slightly.

Claire went on. "I've traced some of the old routing info, telco infrastructure, land holding corps, endowments... and your name came up."

That earned a reaction. Not fear, just the faint tightening around the ranger's jaw. Not denial. Not quite anger. Just memory.

"So you came to the woods to ask questions about a ghost company," Celeste said. "You think you'll find truth here?"

"No," Claire admitted. "But I thought I might find someone who remembers it."

Celeste looked down at the dirt, then back up.

"I didn't work for them," she said carefully. "Not directly."

Claire nodded. "Environmental auditing division. TE Logistics. I found your name on an oversight report from 2007."

A silence opened between them. It was not hostile, just fragile. Claire didn't fill it.

Celeste sighed and walked over to one of the tower's lower support beams. She leaned against it, arms folded.

"They said it was clean energy," she said at last. "That the subsidiary was about carbon credits, reforestation offsets. I believed it. I was twenty-seven. Wanted to make a difference."

Claire stayed quiet.

"They sent me out to survey sites. Forest lots in Montana. A coast parcel in Oregon. One in Panama." Celeste looked away for a moment. "But the numbers never added up. It was like they were using our work to avoid environmental regulation, not comply with it. I filed reports. They went nowhere. I kept copies. Then one day I was told I'd been reassigned except no one told me where. So I walked away."

She looked up at Claire fully for the first time.

"You're the first person who's ever come looking."

Claire swallowed. "I'm sorry."

"Don't be," Celeste said. "I found something better than answers."

Claire tilted her head. "Which is?"

The ranger glanced up at the sky, filtering through the branches above.

"Stillness."

Claire didn't push.

The wind moved through the trees; slow, circular, and higher than it had been when she'd arrived. A few yellow leaves loosened from the canopy and spiralled to the ground. Early for fall. Or maybe just this patch of forest knew something the others didn't.

"Why are you still chasing this?" Celeste asked finally. Her voice wasn't accusatory. Just... tired. "What would happen if you just stopped?"

Claire didn't answer right away. She looked toward the tower. Its silhouette was stark against the blue sky, but it didn't feel menacing. Just... permanent.

"I think if I stopped," she said softly, "I'd always wonder what was left buried. And maybe I could live with that. But I don't think I could look in the mirror and not see someone who chose to stay blind."

Celeste nodded once, as if she'd expected that.

She walked a few steps away and placed a hand on the wide trunk of a pine tree, her palm resting flat against the bark. "You see that?" she said, gesturing to a scar in the trunk, long-healed but still visible. "Lightning strike. Ten years ago. Burned half the canopy. But the roots held."

Claire stepped closer.

"The forest remembers what's been done to it," Celeste said. "But it grows anyway."

Claire stared at the bark. "Do you ever regret walking away?"

The ranger's hand dropped. "Some nights," she said. "I wonder if I did enough. Or if I just took the easy path. But out here.."

She looked upward, where the sky bent around the tower's peak.

"Out here, you're no one. That's the gift. Take it when you can."

Claire breathed that in. It didn't feel like surrender. It felt like an offering.

"But if you keep poking that thing," Celeste said, her eyes turning sharp again, "just know they don't silence you with guns anymore. Not most of the time. They make your life slowly uninhabitable. They erase your career. Turn your friends cold. Twist your own doubts until you self-destruct."

A gust of wind rolled through the clearing colder now. Leaves fell from high above, twirling in silence between them. Claire thought about what Everett said about the tree.

Celeste didn't flinch.

"You strike me as the kind who won't stop anyway," she said.

Claire gave a sad little smile. "You strike me as someone who didn't stop either. Not really."

Celeste nodded, conceding the point.

Then she turned back toward the woods. "The trail back's easier than the climb. But it gets darker quicker than you think."

Claire stood a moment longer while the wind whispered through the trees, and the fire tower creaked faintly overhead, a metal memory holding its ground.

She didn't want to move. Not yet.

There was something about the stillness—the scent of pine, the way the forest swallowed every sound but the wind—that made her want to stay. Pitch a tent. Vanish. Let the world forget her while she remembered how to breathe.

But the light was fading.

And she had questions that wouldn't wait for peace.

Claire exhaled, steadying herself, then turned towards the trail back to her car.

The motel was still. The kind of stillness that didn't feel restful, but paused. As if someone had hit mute on the world just before she pulled into the gravel lot.

Claire stepped out of the car and stood for a moment, fingers tightening around her keys. The wind was wrong, not in speed or direction, but in tone. It didn't rustle the trees. It skimmed past them like a breath held too long.

She walked to the door of her room and hesitated. There was no visible sign of forced entry, no crack in the wood, no jiggled handle. Still, something felt off.

Inside, the air was cooler than she'd left it. The curtains had been drawn slightly wider, letting in more of the outside dusk. She hadn't done that.

Claire set her bag down slowly and turned, scanning everything.

The bed was made. The kettle untouched. Her notes still fanned across the small table by the window.

But the photograph.

It lay face-down on the carpet, near the side of the bed. The photo she'd found in the vault, the one of her father, younger than she ever remembered, dressed in pressed clothes beside men who were not named.

She hadn't left it there. She was certain.

Kneeling, Claire picked it up. A faint fingerprint smeared the corner. She couldn't say for sure it wasn't her own but somehow she knew. Her breath hitched.

"Ada?".

No response.

She turned and opened her laptop. The little green light blinked to life.

Ada, Claire typed quickly. *Were the cameras running? Did you see who came in?*

There was a pause.

Then: *Cameras went offline at 1:42pm. All feeds interrupted. No local footage saved.*

Claire stared at the screen. *Interrupted how?*

Remote intrusion. It wasn't noisy. No backdoor traces. Just… precision. Whoever did this knew exactly what they were doing.

A pulse began to thud behind her eyes. She stood, breathing tightly through her nose.

They wanted me to know, she typed.

Yes. A message. Not violence. Yet.

Claire took two steps back, scanned the room again. Her notebooks were untouched. The drawers not even rifled. They didn't need to steal. They needed to rattle.

You need to leave, Ada said.

I know.

She grabbed her phone and thumbed through her contacts.

Jesse.

The call picked up almost instantly. "Hey. You back from the woods?"

Her voice came out flatter than she intended. "They were in my room."

Silence. Then: "Are you okay?"

"I'm not hurt. But they moved something. Took nothing. Just showed me they could."

"You're not staying there another night."

"I wasn't planning to." She tried to smile. "I was just deciding which ditch to sleep in instead."

"Claire."

His voice was different now. No trace of playfulness. Just a quiet insistence. "Come stay at mine. Please. I'm not asking to be a hero. I just don't want you alone."

She swallowed. "Okay."

"You sure?"

"I'm not. But yes."

"Pack your things. I'll come get you."

"No, I'll drive."

"Still stubborn," he said, but softly.

"I'll be there in fifteen."

She hung up and turned to the room.

The packing didn't take long but it felt like something else entirely. A ritual of departure under pressure. A silent evacuation. Her hands were quick, movements clipped. She swept her notes into a folder, laptop into a satchel, charger cords and phone battery packs thrown in without checking.

She pulled the curtains shut with a firm tug and checked the closet.

Empty.

The pressure hadn't lifted. If anything, it was mounting.

She paused once, looking back at the photo of her father. She'd tucked it between pages in her notebook.

At the door, she turned one last time.

The room was spotless. Ordinary. Forgettable.

But something about the air had changed. It wasn't her room anymore. It belonged to the threat now.

She left the key on the nightstand and stepped out into the evening.

Behind her, the door clicked shut.

The kettle whistled low, then clicked off with a hollow metallic pop.

Claire sat on Jesse's old corduroy couch, arms folded tight across her chest. Her duffel bag leaned against the side table, a corner of a folder of documents peeking out like a warning.

Jesse came back from the kitchen, setting two mismatched mugs on the coffee table.

"Chamomile," he said. "Don't make fun of me. It's what I had."

Claire managed the shadow of a smile. "I'm not here to judge your tea game."

He sat down beside her. Not too close, not too far. Just close enough to be comforting, not smothering. His flannel shirt still smelled like sawdust and soap.

"I checked the locks twice," he said, voice low. "Front and back."

Claire nodded. "Thanks."

They sat in silence for a beat. The only sound was the faint tick of the wall clock above the fireplace. The hum of the fridge in the next room. Everything sounded *louder* here.

Jesse leaned forward, elbows on his knees. "You sure you don't want to report it?"

"I thought about it," she said, wrapping her fingers around the mug. "But nothing was taken. Nothing obvious."

"The photo, though. You said it was moved."

She nodded. "And the cameras the portable ones I had in the motel room. They were offline. Not unplugged. Jammed or remotely disabled. Ada says there's no recovery."

Jesse exhaled slowly. "So, whoever it was… knew what they were doing."

Claire didn't respond at first. Then: "Yeah. They didn't take anything because that wasn't the point."

"What *was* the point?"

She stared into the steam rising from her tea. "To let me know they were there. That they could get in. That they're watching, but not ready to stop me. Not yet."

Jesse's jaw tensed. "Claire.."

"I'm not crazy," she said sharply. Then, softening: "I've been followed. Warned off. Twice now."

She listed them off like pins on a board:

The local cop who issued tickets for her vehicle.

The older sheriff, warning her to stop.

"They weren't arrests. They were warnings."

Jesse didn't interrupt. Just nodded. Absorbing it. Watching her closely.

"And if I file a report," she continued, "where does it go? Same precinct? Same people? Whoever did this... they have reach. And subtlety."

She placed her mug down carefully.

"I think I'm safer here. At least you'd hear someone coming."

Jesse gave a small, grim smile. "This house isn't exactly a fortress."

"No, but it's yours. That's different."

He glanced toward the window. Then back to her. "So what's next?"

Claire leaned back, the couch creaking under her weight. Her voice was quieter now, but steadier.

"I stop looking for symbols," she said. "And I start looking for people."

Jesse frowned slightly, but didn't interrupt.

"They've erased names, buried documents, scattered clues across websites and zoning forms. They scared my uncle into silence. But now I want to know who benefits. Who's still pulling the strings and why it's worth hiding."

Her eyes flicked to the folder in her bag.

"This isn't just history anymore. It's infrastructure. It's current. Whatever the Order is it still *functions*. And if it's still functioning, someone's still *running* it."

She took a breath. "And then there's my father."

Jesse tilted his head slightly.

"I found a photo," she said. "My dad years before the accident, when I was still a child. It was there in plain sight."

She looked away. "I always thought my uncle was the unusual one after finding the letter. The academic who got in too deep but could not outrun dementia. But now I wonder if my father… if he knew. Or worse if he was part of it."

Jesse's face softened. "Claire, it could have been any connection."

"I'm not saying he was guilty," she said quickly. "But I need to know what they were all protecting. What they were *afraid* I'd find."

A moment passed.

"I think they moved the photo in the motel because they wanted me off-balance. But they made a mistake."

Jesse raised an eyebrow. "What mistake?"

Claire looked up at him. "They reminded me I have skin in the game."

He went still.

"I'm not just chasing ghosts anymore," she said. "I want names. Faces. Bank records. Land deeds. Whoever's still running this thing, I'm going to find them. And I want to know why someone like my father ended up in their shadows."

Jesse leaned back, rubbing the back of his neck.

"Alright," he said finally. "Then you stay here. For as long as you need."

Claire met his eyes. "You sure?"

"I wouldn't offer if I wasn't. And besides…" he hesitated. "I still remember you from before. You were stubborn as hell even then. I don't think anyone could talk you out of this."

She cracked the faintest smile. "Thanks?"

"I mean it as a compliment."

The clock ticked again. The tea cooled. Outside, a gust of wind brushed through the trees, nudging the loose gutter on Jesse's porch into a soft metallic *tap… tap… tap.*

Claire reached into her bag, unzipped the outer pocket, and pulled out her laptop. Flipped it open. Ada's interface glowed in the dim light.

She typed:

Are we secure?

A pause.

For now. You chose well. His walls are thicker than they look.

Claire exhaled. "Ada says we're good."

"Creepy," Jesse muttered. But not unkindly.

"Comforting," Claire corrected.

Then she added, almost absently: "You don't have to stay up with me, you know."

Jesse stood slowly, stretching his back. "Nah. I'll be around. Join me when you're ready. Holler if you hear the goat again."

Claire blinked. "That was *one time.*"

He chuckled, stepping down the hall toward the main bedroom. "Still. Might be our unofficial mascot now. Guardian of weird clues and friendly AI. But definitely shout if you see bigfoot."

Claire looked back to the screen. The cursor blinked.

You okay? Ada typed.

Claire didn't answer right away. Then she typed:

Not sure. But I'm not leaving.

The house was still. No footsteps. No voices. Just the soft hum of the fridge and the muted scratch of Claire's fingers on the laptop trackpad.

She sat at the kitchen table, sleeves pushed up, hair loose, eyes half-lit by the glow of the screen. A half-empty mug sat forgotten by her elbow, its steam long gone.

Lines of code scrolled past. Then stopped.

Claire Ada wrote, the cursor blinking once.

Claire sat up straighter. *What is it?*

A brief pause.

One of the shell corporations, Meridian Crop Holdings. It was dormant. But activity resumed three weeks ago. It owns land forty miles southeast of here. Remote, forested. The parcel is listed as agricultural use, but satellite data shows no visible crops.

Claire frowned. *Anything else on the property?*

No public utilities. No road signage. But power draw exists — off-grid. Nighttime thermal patterns suggest human presence.

Claire didn't say anything for a moment. She just stared at the screen. Then typed:

Do you think it's them?

Ada's response came quickly.

It aligns with other documents and obfuscation. Obscure front.
Rural location. Digital silence.
A quiet place to keep quiet things.

Claire felt something shift in her chest. Not fear, not exactly. But clarity. A shape forming in the mist.

She rested her fingers on the keyboard. Then slowly typed:

Do you think I should go?

There was a longer pause this time.

Then, on the screen:

You already decided that.

Claire exhaled. A quiet, private truth she hadn't admitted, not even to herself.

She glanced toward the hallway. Jesse wasn't back yet. Or maybe he was already asleep. Either way, she didn't call out. She turned back to the screen.

You're not just guessing anymore, are you? she said aloud.

The cursor blinked.

Then:

No.

Claire leaned back in the chair, arms crossed loosely.
When did that start happening?

What?

You answering before I ask.

There was a pause. Then Ada replied:
You've stopped hiding the question.

Claire sat with that. It wasn't wrong.
I guess we've been through a lot, haven't we?

You've changed.

She let out a breath, not quite a laugh.
"So have you."

For a moment, neither spoke. Just the hum of the fan,
and the quiet rhythm of the cursor blinking.

Then, Ada typed:

*This location, you'll need to be careful. No signal range. Bring a
second power source. And leave a note somewhere. Even if you
don't want to.*

Noted.

She moved to close the lid, but hesitated. One last line.

Thanks, Ada.

Another pause. Then:

You're welcome, Claire.

She shut the laptop gently like she was letting something sleep and sat in the hush of the kitchen for a moment longer.

Then she stood, and the chair creaked softly behind her.

The night didn't feel quite so quiet now.

The next evening adventure called. Claire pulled off the highway and turned down an unmarked fire road, the kind half-swallowed by trees and forgotten by maps. She followed it for a few minutes, tires crunching over frost-bitten gravel and broken twigs, until the undergrowth thickened and the canopy closed in overhead. Then she cut the engine and rolled the vehicle behind a thicket of bare scrub brush, out of sight from the main road.

Claire was alone. Despite the risk something in her told her not to tell Jesse; perhaps concern he would talk her out of it, perhaps something else.

A few stubborn crickets chirped in the undergrowth. Beyond that, nothing but wind and the faint rustle of dry weeds shifting in the low light.

She pulled the keys from the ignition and slipped them into her coat pocket. No cell signal. No visible signs of life. Just a narrow service gate, part of the old barbed perimeter fencing that once kept livestock in, or maybe something else out.

She moved on foot now, boots crunching faintly on scattered stone. A long, narrow trail curved inward toward a tree-lined depression where the land dipped slightly. Through the branches, the top of a red tin roof revealed itself. The barn.

Claire crouched as she approached the perimeter, hand resting on her thigh, breath even. One small building sat just off to the left. It was a farmhouse, two stories, white siding gone grey with age. One window upstairs glowed amber. The curtain didn't move.

She stayed clear of it.

The barn door was padlocked, but the side panel near the rear was loose. She wedged her shoulder into the gap and slipped inside, careful not to disturb the hanging tools or stacked crates that lined the walls. The air smelled like mould, dust, and engine oil.

At the centre of the barn sat a large shipping container, matte grey, the kind used for cross-country freight. A generator hummed nearby, silent to the outside, but a low mechanical breath in the quiet space.

Claire stepped up the metal ramp and pushed the container door. Unlocked. It creaked open slow, like something exhaling.

Inside, a foldaway table was set up against the right wall. On it: a money-counting machine, unplugged but still dustless. Two cardboard boxes sat beside it, one filled with fresh rubber bands, the other with black nylon duffel bags identical to the ones she'd seen at the butcher shop.

To the left, a metal cabinet, unmarked. She opened it: rows of hanging folders, unlabelled, loose papers stuffed in at odd angles. One folder stuck out, half-burned along the edge. She pulled it free. Inside: a sheaf of printed invoices, all bearing the name *TE Holdings* and a string of defunct LLCs. One listed a vehicle maintenance contract for a trucking firm in Kansas likely a front.

Claire snapped photos, wide shots, detail closeups. She moved efficiently, trying not to breathe too loudly.

In the corner, above the doorframe, a CCTV camera faced the interior. She froze.

But the LED was dark. No power. Maybe disconnected. Or maybe it had already seen enough.

Her eyes swept the rest of the container. It was clean, functional, no clutter. Just a system humming quietly below the radar.

They're still using this, she thought. This isn't abandoned. It's active.

Claire tucked the invoice into her jacket and turned to leave. Her hand was on the door when she paused.

From the far side of the barn, something flickered.

She crouched down and peered through the slats.

Headlights.

A car was pulling in. Not fast but deliberate. Black
SUV, newer model. No plates.

She ducked low, heart thudding now, and slid out the
rear panel the way she came in. Behind the barn was a
pile of old hay bales, some half-rotted, stacked against
the fencing. She slid behind them just as the SUV
rolled to a stop.

Five minutes passed.

Then, a second vehicle. This one a silver town car,
clean, government plates glinting faintly in the twilight.
The door opened. Two men stepped out. One in a
black coat, tall. The other..

Claire's gut clenched.

Senator Harold Kinney. Same slicked-back grey hair,
same slow gait she remembered from interviews and
C-SPAN hearings. His face looked thinner in person.
Harder. No smile.

She knew the name from Fordham lectures. Knew the
endless news articles he appeared in; always attached to
something quietly powerful, never controversial. The
kind of man who existed long in the bureaucracy of
DC.

Kinney and the other man walked toward the barn
entrance, stopping just outside. Claire didn't dare move,

only pressing herself deeper into the bale stack, one frozen hand still wrapped around her cracked phone.

They spoke low, but not quietly enough.

"Funding holds through Q4", the unknown man said. "The ledger's clean. No leaks".

"This site's our quiet wash", Kinney replied. "The rest run offshore, but this one... this one's friendly. Local eyes. No noise".

A pause. Then

"I hear the girl has been looking into things".

Claire froze.

"Make sure we get rid of that Ashridge Hollow Archive. Quietly. Tonight. Make it look like an accident. Some sort of electrical wiring issue".

The man nodded. "We'll send the cleanup crew later".

Claire's heart thundered in her chest.

Kinney continued, his voice dry:

"And the girl?"

"She's noise. Emotional. The moment she realizes there's no door to knock on, she'll go home. They always do. And if she doesn't, well we know how to handle that."

Kinney said nothing for a moment. Then turned toward the SUV.

"Let's not give her time to find those doors.".

He climbed in without looking back.

Claire's hands were shaking now, the phone slick in her palm. The recording was still running, the faint red bar pulsing on-screen, caught mid-conversation.

She didn't move. Couldn't. Not until the silver town car backed out the way it came. Not until the SUV followed five minutes later, headlights dimmed as they pulled away down the fire road.

Only then did she breathe again.

They weren't just protecting old secrets.

They were cleaning house.

And she didn't know whether to be thankful or disappointed… to be dismissed as *emotional*.

The night had deepened. Whatever light was left in the sky had bled out behind the hills, leaving the air colder, heavier.

Claire moved cautiously, boots crunching on dead leaves as she skirted the barn's rear. She kept to the shadows, retracing her steps to the fire road.

One photo. One recording. One half-burned invoice in her jacket.

You have what you need, she told herself. *Get out.*

She was thirty feet from the tree line when something shifted behind her.

A footstep. Too close.

Claire turned fast and caught the sharp glint of a flashlight beam cutting through the dark. A figure stepped out from behind the fence line, lean frame silhouetted against the barn.

Not one of the men from earlier.

He wore a plain jacket, heavy boots, and no badge. His flashlight dipped for a second, catching her face.

He froze.

Then narrowed his eyes.

"Who are you?"

Claire didn't answer.

He stepped forward, fast. "You're not usually here. Who the hell are you?"

She turned to bolt but he closed the distance in two strides. His hand clamped around her arm, dragging her sideways, hard. Her phone slipped from her grip and smashed against the rocks.

Claire twisted, shoving him back, but he was stronger. He slammed her into the base of the barn wall, his breath hot, sour.

 "You're not supposed to be here."

Her elbow shot back caught him in the ribs. He grunted, stumbled, then grabbed for her again.

She spotted it near the base of the wall; an old metal rod, half-buried in the dirt. Maybe a tire iron, maybe part of a fence bracket. She didn't think.

Claire lunged, grabbed it with both hands, and swung hard.

The impact echoed like bone on steel. The man dropped instantly, crumpled sideways into the grass, limbs twitching once before going still.

Claire stood over him, panting, the rod still in her hand.

Her heartbeat pounded in her ears.

She backed away fast. Her knees were trembling. Her jacket torn. A line of blood smeared across her wrist, not deep, but enough to sting.

She reached the tree line in a sprint, breath raw, limbs aching. The car was still there, half-concealed, dark and waiting.

Inside, she fumbled with the keys. Got the engine going on the second try. Gravel scattered behind her as she pulled out, headlights off until she hit the first bend.

Only once she'd put three miles between herself and that barn did she risk glancing down at her phone.

The screen was spiderwebbed. The app still open, but the recording indicator was frozen. No timer.

No guarantee the audio saved.

She didn't cry.

Didn't scream.

She just kept driving past the broken fences, past the silence, past the point of safety.

Claire sat cross-legged on the floor, the broken phone disassembled beside her on the rug. Laptop was open, Ada's interface flickering faintly on the screen. The room smelled like antiseptic and dust; Jesse had helped patch the cut on her wrist, the stern look of disappointment.

He stood a few feet away, arms folded, gaze fixed on the laptop. His jaw was tight.

Ada's text crawled across the screen:

Attempting recovery... File fragments located. Estimated data loss: 87%.

Claire exhaled slowly.

Partial image sequence preserved. Audio corrupted beyond repair.

She leaned back against the couch, hands resting in her lap.

Jesse broke the silence.

"You didn't tell me where you were going."

Claire didn't look up. "I didn't think you'd approve."

"You're right. I wouldn't have."

He moved toward the coffee table, picked up the cracked phone gently.

"And this? You could've been" He stopped. Let the thought hang.

Claire met his eyes for a second. "But I wasn't."

He ran a hand through his hair, then dropped onto the armchair across from her.

"I'm not asking for control, Claire. Just... trust. You don't have to go through all this alone."

She nodded once. But didn't answer.

On the screen, Ada added quietly:

One document partially intact. Exporting.

Claire clicked, opening the file. The same fake invoice from earlier charred along the edge, TE Holdings watermarked faintly at the top. Not enough to publish. But enough to remember.

Jesse's voice was softer now.

"You look like hell."

"Thanks."

"I mean it kindly."

She gave a half-smile. Just barely.

Then silence returned. Not angry. Just full of things unsaid.

Outside, the wind pressed against the windows like it wanted in.

That night, Claire slept like a body pulled from water. Not rested, just heavy. She didn't remember curling into Jesse's arms, only the warmth. And the absence of noise.

By morning, the pain returned.

The cut on her arm throbbed. Her ribs ached from the scuffle. Her mind kept looping back to the man's face, not scared, just surprised. Like she wasn't who he expected.

Jesse was in the shower. The soft hum of the bathroom fan carried down the hallway.

Claire stood in the kitchen, one hand on the counter, eyes on the floor. The sunlight made the tile look too clean.

Then his phone buzzed, screen lighting up with a soft chime.

She didn't reach for it right away. Just stared. Long enough for instinct to take over.

She picked it up. Locked. She shouldn't. She knew that. But her fingers moved anyway. Out of instinct. Out of something older.

She entered his birthday.

It opened.

The messages were ordinary. A few from clients, one from a cousin. Then she saw a contact labelled only as "J."

Nothing recent but there was a deleted message still visible in the Recently Removed folder.

She tapped.

Money's transferred. She needs to stop. Persuade her to leave.

The timestamp hit her harder than the words.

It was the night of the firepit.

The night he'd laughed with her. Listened. The night she'd told him about the scars. About the dark place.

She didn't hear the water stop. Didn't notice him entering the room.

"Claire?"

She turned slowly, still holding the phone.

"What is this."

He froze. "Claire.."

"Don't lie."

He looked at the ground. Swallowed hard.

"It was supposed to be nothing. Just keep you distracted. Keep you from digging too hard."

She said nothing.

"I didn't know I'd actually feel anything. But I did. Claire, I do. That was before."

She didn't raise her voice.

"So while I was telling you about the darkest moments of my life... you were just earning your silence."

He didn't deny it. Couldn't.

Claire didn't say anything else.
She set the phone down on the counter gently, like it might break then walked past him, her shoulders squared and her face unreadable. Grabbing her bag and laptop.

She didn't slam the door.

But the sound of it closing felt louder than anything else he'd ever heard.

Jesse stood frozen for a moment, staring at the space she had just left. Then the weight of it all crashed down.

He turned and slammed his fist into the kitchen wall. Not hard enough to break the drywall, but enough to feel it in his bones. The echo filled the house.

Then he slid down the same wall, back against it, breathing heavy.

His head dropped into his hands. Tears forming, before he wiped them away. He stayed there in the silence, alone in the dark. And for the first time in a long time, Jesse Calder didn't know how to fix what he'd broken.

Claire pulled over a few minutes after leaving town, the Sign 'Welcome to Ashridge Hollow' well in the rearview mirror. Claire locked the sedan, and opened her laptop. The light from the screen lit her tired face.

Ada appeared.

Claire?

It's over Ada, she whispered. He was working with them.

A pause.

I'm sorry. You deserved better.

Claire said nothing. She opened a folder on her desktop, pictures from the Fall Festival. One of her and Jesse laughing, arms around each other.

She hovered for a moment.

Then selected the entire folder.

Delete.

Gone.

She closed the laptop, started up the engine.

No tears. No words.

Just the hum of the engine as she went forward on NY-8 south.

The road curved gently east, headlights carving through mist that hadn't yet decided if it was fog or rain.

Claire drove in silence.

No music. No podcasts. Just the low hum of tires and the occasional hiss of wet asphalt beneath her wheels. Forest blurred past on both sides, bare trees, rust-coloured leaves clinging to the last of October.

Her wrist ached where the skin had split. The cut was small, but she kept pressing her thumb against it, grounding herself in the sting.

She'd driven this route once before. Years ago. With her father.

Back when the world still felt like it operated on laws, even the unspoken ones.

Now?

Now the most powerful man she'd ever seen in person had talked about burning an archive like it was a broken lightbulb. No hesitation. No doubt.

And Jesse...

She blinked hard. Focused on the centre line.

What hurt most wasn't the betrayal. It was how normal he made her feel for a while.

And how much she had wanted that.

A green sign flashed by overhead: Albany 42 Miles. NYC 168.

She pressed her foot down just a little harder.

Home was still far off.

But it was waiting.

The key turned in the lock with a soft metallic sigh. Claire stepped inside her apartment in Norwood, closing the door behind her with a quiet thud. The hallway light buzzed faintly overhead. Familiar. Unchanged.

Eggroll was already padding toward her, tail high, meowing like she'd been gone a decade.

"Hey, menace", she whispered, crouching down. He bumped his head against her knee and purred like a small engine.

From the kitchen, Citra emerged in oversized sweats, a bowl of popcorn in her hands.

"You didn't call", she said.

Claire set her bag down. "I couldn't".

"No need to explain", Citra replied. "I queued up something dumb and overly sweet. You need emotional carbs".

Claire gave the ghost of a smile and sank into the couch. Eggroll leapt up beside her, curling instantly into her lap.

The screen flickered to life. Some mid-90s rom-com with questionable fashion and aggressively bad lines.

They watched for a few minutes in silence. Claire's breathing slowed. Her hand rested on Eggroll's back.

Then slowly, silently, the tears came.

She didn't sob. Just let them fall.

Citra reached over and pulled her in. No words. Just held her.

Eggroll chirped and climbed higher, plopping awkwardly across Claire's chest.

Claire let out a short, broken laugh between the tears.

"Traitor", she muttered, smiling.

Citra smiled softly. "He likes you damaged. Makes you warmer".

Claire didn't reply. Just a small smile between the tears.

Outside, the city moved on. But here, in this small pocket of stillness, something held.

Not fixed. Not healed.

Just... *held.*

A few days later, Claire sat down at her desk. She was back home, finally. The comfort of her own apartment, the streetlights outside casting a dull amber glow through the curtains.

Her tea had long gone cold, but she didn't care.

She powered on the pc, and the screen blinked to life.

Ada's cursor flickered once, then typed automatically into the command bar, their nightly ritual. Open the tabs. Scan the feeds. Keep digging.

Initializing session...
Loading top regional news sources, security bulletins, and monitored search terms...

The first browser tab bloomed open. A headline in muted serif font stared back at her.

Private Jet Registered to CEO of Flynn Botanicals Lost Off Bahamas Coast

Claire blinked. The subheading loaded a second later.

Sarah Flynn, entrepreneur and philanthropist, presumed dead following storm-related crash. Search suspended due to deteriorating conditions.

Her fingers hovered above the trackpad but didn't move.

Ada's cursor pulsed.

Storm intensity was moderate. Cause of crash under review.

Claire leaned back slightly, exhaling, not shocked. Not exactly. Just… cold inside.

She hadn't told anyone about the call. Hadn't mentioned Sarah's name out loud since that night. The only trace was buried in Ada's logs.

A pause.

Then Ada typed:

Nothing else unusual on the feed tonight. Shall I continue loading tabs?

Claire nodded absently. *Yeah. Go ahead.*

Another flicker of silence. Then:

We're not done yet, are we?

Claire didn't answer right away. Just stared at the headline. Still open. Still waiting.

Then, quietly
"No. We aren't."

Thank you for reading *The Quiet Order*.

If you enjoyed the story, you can explore more of our work: eerie fiction, thoughtful nonfiction, and books of hope at:

farbellum.com

You'll also find updates, future releases, and ways to support the next chapter.

Built by hand. Written with care. Farbellum Press.